Mother Wants a Horse

BOOKS BY DIANA WALKER

*Mother Wants a Horse**
The Hundred Thousand Dollar Farm
Never Step on an Indian's Shadow
*The Year of the Horse**

**Available in Harper Trophy paperback edition*

Diana Walker

MOTHER WANTS A HORSE

A HARPER TROPHY BOOK

HARPER & ROW, PUBLISHERS

New York, Hagerstown, San Francisco, London

For my fellow riders
Daphne Cargill and Jean Douglas
and for Wapiti Kitti,
a Very Special Horse

Mother Wants a Horse

Printed in the United States of America.
For information address Harper & Row, Publishers, Inc., 10 East 53rd Street, New York, N.Y. 10022. Published simultaneously in Canada by Fitzhenry & Whiteside Limited, Toronto.
ISBN 0-06-440101-4

First published under the Abelard-Schuman imprint of Thomas Y. Crowell Company in 1978.
First Harper Trophy edition, 1979.

Contents

Othello

FATHER was angry, and when he was angry, he boomed. It was the only word to describe it. Although he was a writer, mostly of television scripts, his close association with actors had rubbed off on him, and everything he did seemed twice as large as life, as though he were perennially play-acting. The trouble was, this wasn't a script; it was my life, and I wasn't doing well at all. The only line I had had so far was "But, Dad," and I had repeated it so often it had gone stale. Meanwhile, he was in great form, upstaging me like mad, pacing up and down my bedroom with great strides, his luxurious beard bristling in every hair.

"Joanna, I am humiliated—humiliated to the core! The Longfellows are an extremely literate family. They have produced writers, poets, and thinkers of the highest caliber. We are a scholarly family. We have always prized brains above brawn. And what do I find when I come home from the city?" At the far end of the room he swiveled around and nailed me with a look of utmost horror. "My own daughter"—he paused for effect and clamped a hand to his brow—"failed in English! I cannot . . . I just cannot believe it!"

"But, Dad—"

"Don't answer me back!" That wasn't fair since I hadn't been able yet to get a word in edgeways. He was off again, playing the part of the aggrieved parent to the full. "Do I deserve this? Haven't I given in to your every whim, encouraged your riding, attended your shows, cheered you on, in fact given you every support—and this is how you repay me, by failing in English? Joanna, I have no words at all. I am speechless!"

I didn't think the description was very apt, but I hadn't the courage to say so. Anyway at that moment the bedroom door opened inward, the result of too much pressure upon it, and my young brothers, Maxwell and Julian, who were nine and thirteen respectively, fell into the room. My father's wrath was temporarily diverted from me, and I blessed Maxwell and Julian, something I rarely did.

"Aha!" said Father scathingly. "Listening at doors, eh? A very commendable practice. No doubt, you are readying yourselves for a career in the Secret Service?"

Maxwell was not at all awed by my father's sarcasm, being a smaller edition of him and able to give as good as he got. "We weren't listening at doors," he said, making himself comfortable on the bed. "We were just passing, and the door blew open. It's all those drafts in the corridor. You know what Grandma said."

Father turned red in the face. We had been renting our grandmother's house since last spring when she had remarried. Before that, we had never been able to settle anywhere, moving from apartment to apartment and constantly disrupting our lives. No one had been more surprised than we when Father adapted to country life as though born to it, commuting the sixty miles or so to Toronto to the television studios when necessary, but spending the rest of the time playing the country squire, with grandiose plans for improving Grandma's old house, which so far had come to nothing.

Maxwell's remark touched a sore spot. Before Grandma had married Mr. Archer and moved across to the back road, she had warned my father that the house needed a lot of repairs and that our heating bills would be enormous, if he didn't get cracking and putty up a few holes, instead of dreaming up sunken gardens, glassed-in conservatories, and sweeping green lawns gliding down to the barn and the muck pile.

Father spluttered a bit but rallied gamely. "That's as it may be. Meanwhile, might I ask what you two are doing, or would that be a violation of your privacy?"

Maxwell's sidekick, Julian, who had joined him on the bed, said in his usual practical manner, "We can hear you outside anyway, so we might just as well stay here and listen in comfort."

"Out!" exploded Father. "Out!"

They sighed and left. We could hear them clumping down the stairs, kicking the woodwork, and running their fingers down the bannister rails. But they had served a purpose. Having been exposed to them, I didn't seem so bad to

Father. He eyed me sorrowfully and sat down heavily on the bed.

"It won't do, Joanna. Ever since Mr. Holmes discovered your riding abilities and took you on as his protegée, your whole life has been horses. You think and dream horses. You even neigh in your sleep. Your schoolwork has gone to the devil. English happens to be a compulsory subject, I suppose you realize."

I did, only too well; but the day before the exam I had won two red ribbons—first prizes—for Holmwood Farms, and I had been training so hard for the show I had practically fallen asleep during the exam. I tried to explain this.

"It wasn't my fault, Daddy. It was an important show, and I needed the training. Both Jim and Mr. Holmes said I did. If I'm going to be good enough for the Royal Horse Show in November, I've got to do all these shows. You know that. You were proud enough when Queenie and I took two firsts. You were boasting to everyone that I was your daughter, and you didn't seem to care then whether I was literate or not." I was warming up now, full of self-righteousness. "You even suggested to Mr. Holmes that we have a party over at Holmwood House to celebrate. It wasn't my idea."

All the same it had been a wonderful party. John Holmes had come up specially from Guelph, where he was training to be a vet, and we had danced together and walked under the stars through the rose gardens at the back of the house. Taking off our shoes, we had dangled our aching feet in the swimming pool, and John had told me that all the girls at veterinary college tended to look like horses and that it was nice to be with a girl who looked like a girl again. To me, all horses were beautiful, something that I wasn't, although I do have nice long dark hair; still, I didn't particularly want to look like a horse. I could still remember my reaction the first time I met John when I had been a tongue-tied fifteen-year-old staying with Grandma. He had looked so handsome and splendid riding Queenie that I had felt like a clod. Who could have guessed that fifteen months later I would be riding Queenie at all the shows, and the big house at Holmwood Farms would be a second home to me? Sometimes I still felt unreal about it all. I looked across at my father timidly. His booming mood was over, but I knew him too well to expect it to end there.

He was being reasonable now. Being reasonable with Father meant speaking very slowly and distinctly as though you were half witted.

"Of course I'm proud of you, Joanna. Ever since John decided he didn't like competitive riding, and Mr. Holmes saw in you a prospective candidate to take his place, you have excelled yourself. A year ago last spring you had never been on a horse; now by sheer hard work and determination you are good enough to qualify for the Royal. However"—he squashed my self-satisfied smile with a stony look—"there are other things in the world more important than achievement in the equestrian field, and one of those is a good education. You are going to take that English exam again and pass it. Do you understand?"

"Yes, Daddy," I complied meekly.

"Your mother has been making inquiries about a coach

for you. Apparently there is a Mrs. Williams, an ex-teacher, who has recently bought the stone cottage two miles down the road. I talked with this lady this morning on the phone, and she is willing to give you special coaching in English on Saturday mornings during the summer vacation. Henceforth I hope you will apply yourself as diligently to your lessons as you do to your riding, particularly since this is costing me money." He stood up from the bed and sighed, his distasteful duty done. "Just don't let me down again. I don't want a brainless ninny for a daughter even if she can sit a horse with the best of them."

I stared at him aghast as he made for the door. "But, Daddy, I can't! Not Saturday mornings!"

He turned, brows arching in exaggeration. "And why not, pray?"

"Because I work at Holmwood Farms Saturday mornings! It's the only money I get." I glowered at him darkly. "*You* never give us any!" That was true. We never seemed to be able to make ends meet like other families, so instead of allowances we got IOUs. By now we had so many IOUs that Maxwell had suggested papering the sleeping porch with them as a gentle reminder to Father and to give him a guilt complex. It wasn't very successful, however, since Maxwell and Julian had their beds there, along with a collection of reptiles, rodents, and revolting-looking insects in glass bottles, and Father tended to avoid the sleeping porch like the plague. The only money we had for our personal use was what we could earn ourselves, and my Saturday morning job at Holmwood Farms, mucking out barns and exercising the horses, was precious to me.

Father was not touched by my wails of protest. "I'm sorry, Joanna, but that's the only time Mrs. Williams can take you. You'll have to ask Jim if you can work Saturday afternoons instead."

"But Mr. Holmes coaches me on Saturday afternoon. And what about the shows coming up? They're always on Saturday afternoon or Sunday!"

My father was totally unimpressed. "There's no more to be said, Joanna. A little self-denial won't hurt you. Perhaps it'll make you pull up your socks in future where your studies are concerned."

Adamant, he went out of my room and closed the door so that my pleadings fell on deaf ears. Desperately I thought about appealing to my mother, but she hadn't been too happy about my failing in English, either. It could set my schooling back a whole year, and no matter how well I rode, that was all they could think about.

I sat down and contemplated this tragedy which had overtaken me. A sixteen-year-old girl had to have some money of her own. I needed a new bathing suit, and my last year's shorts were threadbare and indecent. My sneakers had flapping soles that tripped me up at every step, and two strings on my tennis racket were broken. I had no decent clothes at all. I would become dowdy and frumpish and revert back to my insecure self again. John would lose interest in me, and even the girls at the veterinary college would begin to look good to him.

"Damn!" I said. "Blast!" I kicked the wastebasket viciously across the room, aging our fat cat, Blob, who was snoozing in the sunshine, by about ten years. I ran down the stairs and stormed out of the house just as my eighteen-year-old sister Margaret was entering with her latest substitute boyfriend. Her true love, Wallace Pindlebury, was attending art college in Toronto, and Margaret needed substitutes to keep her hand in. This one was six foot tall with a face like a cherub and two words in his vocabulary, "Yup" and "Nope." He worked for his father at the local feed mill, and he leaked little trails of grain from his pockets and shoes wherever he went, and smelled of malt. His name was Hamilton Schumacher. Margaret fell in love with names, not people.

"Watch it!" she said sharply; then noticing my expression, "I suppose Dad broke the news to you."

I gave her my best imitation of a snarl, and she said, "Naughty, naughty! Temper, temper! Doesn't she look cute when she's mad, Ham?"

"Yup," said Hamilton Schumacher, wafting malt in my direction.

I was hardly ever in the mood for them, but particularly not at this moment. All I wanted to do was jump on a horse and gallop away into infinity, venting my fury to the winds, and woe betide anyone who got in my way.

"Excuse me," I said icily. "If you're from outer space, you'll have to come back later. I have an appointment with Queenie."

Of course, I could have taken Horse, but she only had two speeds—dead slow and stop. She was really Mr. Archer's horse, but her foal, Horse the Second, was Grandma's present to us in celebration of her marriage to Mr. Archer, and so we were looking after both Horse and her colt until Horse the Second was old enough to be on his own. Horse was the most lovable old horse in the world, but so lazy that when she was tired, she leaned on whatever happened to be in the vicinity, sooner than make the effort to lie down. Horse the Second was leggy and adorable, with a curly forelock and saucy tail. He could kick up his heels with the best of them. One day he might race the wind with me, but I couldn't wait that long. They came loping up to the fence and whinnied at me as I ran past them, but I had nothing for them today. I jumped the gate to Holmwood Farms and dashed across the rolling fields to the barns and paddocks behind the house. My anger seethed and grew inside me all the way as I thought how unjustly I had been treated.

It was lunchtime, and the large complex of farm buildings was deserted. That suited me fine, since I didn't particularly want to talk to anyone, least of all to Jim Stiles, who was foreman and trainer at Holmwood Farms. I was very fond of Jim, whose personal coaching had brought me to the attention of Mr. Holmes, and started me on my riding career; but he had the disconcerting habit whenever I blew my top of making me feel about three feet tall, by being quietly and gently rational and speaking to me as though I were a child. I didn't want to be treated like a child today. I had had enough of that already.

It was one thing, however, to visualize myself leaping on a horse and taking off in a flurry of dust to disappear over the horizon, and quite another in actual practice. By the time I had located Queenie in her paddock, brought her into the barn, and tacked her up, I was beginning to have second thoughts about what I was doing. Queenie was a beautiful sorrel hunter, the prize-winning mare of Holmwood Farms, and she was valuable. We stood looking at each other, and it was almost as though Jim were at my elbow saying to me, "So you want to take Queenie outside and ride her recklessly to satisfy your own feeling of frustration, do you, Joanna? And what if she stumbles and falls? What if she breaks a leg? What happens to the Royal then, and to Mr. Holmes's trust in you? Why don't you be your age?"

It was no good. I couldn't do it. My impulsiveness had almost been my downfall on several occasions. I still wanted to jump on a horse and ride without caution until my anger was spent, but I couldn't jeopardize Queenie or my position at Holmwood Farms by doing something stupid. All the horses at Holmwood Farms were registered hunters, all of them valuable. And then I remembered Othello.

Othello was part-Clyde, part-thoroughbred, a big sturdy black horse with an intelligent face and a look of strength about him. He was not part of the stable. A friend of Mr. Holmes's who had moved back to the city had owned him, and Mr. Holmes was boarding him until a new owner could be found. Othello was not valuable in the way that Queenie and the others were, but he was a fine spirited horse, and I needed him right now. Queenie gave me a funny look as I untacked her again and took her back to the paddock, but she was probably used to the crazy ways of humans by now. With the saddle and bridle over my arm, I went to look for Othello. He was in a small enclosure all by himself, and he was pacing up and down with a look in his eye that said he didn't like the confining fence one bit.

"All right, fellow," I said coaxingly, holding out my hand. "I'll give you a run for your money. Come on, good boy!"

He came with no trouble, almost as though he could read my thoughts and was already galloping through the clover-scented fields, free as a bird on this bright sunny morning. I had to stand on a rise to mount him, and it was like sitting on top of the world in a comfortable armchair, he was so broad and well padded. I walked him out of the paddock and out of sight of the barns and house, getting used to the feel of him. Then, when the back forty stretched ahead of me, I dug in my heels and let him go, first at a canter, then at a hand gallop.

I had never been allowed to race Queenie, and it was a new experience for me, the sudden gathering of power, the thundering of hoofs on the turf, the heady sensation of unchecked speed. We took the fence at the end of the field as though it were nonexistent. Othello was enjoying himself tremendously. I doubt if I could have pulled him up if I had wanted to, he was so strong, but I was not in the least bit apprehensive. He was so easy to sit, I could just relax and enjoy it. Now I could forget my troubles, my anger, and my frustration. No one could get me down, not Joanna Longfellow, candidate for the Royal Horse Show, prospective Olympic champion! Watch out, world. I was invincible!

Beyond Holmwood Farms stretched acres of newly

forested land, with trees too small to impede our progress and scattered clumps of bushes which we avoided easily. I was too exhilarated to care much where Othello was taking me. He would tire himself in his own time, and he seemed perfectly capable of looking after himself.

"Faster, you big beautiful thing!" I called to him, leaning low on his neck—and then, too late, I saw the tree! It was a huge maple, standing alone among all the seedling trees, its branches making a great canopy about it right in the path of Othello's stride. I tried to swerve him, but he had a hard mouth, and the bit made no impression at all. There was nothing for it but to duck, only I was perched up a bit too high. A branch slapped in my face, brushing me backward as if I were of no more consequence than a fly. Somersaulting over Othello's tail, I saw the ground coming up to meet me, and I remember vaguely wondering if Othello would keep on going without me, and marveling how I could have such an inborn talent for goofing everything up. Then there was the thud of impact, the countryside turned upside down, and everything went black.

The Williams Family

I COULDN'T have been out for more than a second or so because I became aware of footsteps running through the grass and a voice saying anxiously, "Wow, she fell like a stone! Do you think she's unconscious?"

A second voice close to my ear answered, "I don't know, but she ought never to be out alone with a horse. She must be a beginner. Did you see how she headed straight for that tree?"

I was incensed. I wanted to tell the voice that I was Joanna Longfellow, winner of seven red ribbons, and that I was going to ride in the Royal Horse Show in November for Holmwood Farms, which just happened to be one of the most important breeding stables in southern Ontario. I would have done so, too, except for one slight handicap—I couldn't breathe. There seemed to be a ton weight sitting on my chest. Gingerly I opened my eyes and saw two wide-eyed, pointed little faces peering down at me. Both had short brown hair cut in bangs just above their eyebrows, and they could have been twins except that one appeared to be a couple of inches taller than the other. "She seems to be coming around," said the older of the two with relief in her voice. "Are you all right?"

I was so badly winded, I could only grunt. I moved my head painfully and was thankful to see Othello standing a little way off. He looked at me apologetically as if to say, "Sorry about that. We were having such fun, too." I realized I needn't have worried about him. He was big and strong and powerful, but there wasn't a mean bone in his body. The only trouble with him was that he needed glasses.

With an effort I managed to raise myself on my elbow. The older girl helped to support me while the other hopped around nervously, saying, "Shall I go and get Mother? Maybe she's broken something."

I felt as though I had broken everything, but a quick survey of my arms and legs seemed to show them all to be there and in one piece. "I'm okay," I managed to blurt out. "Just a bit winded, that's all. Sorry to have scared you."

"That's all right," said the older girl. "I'm Dinah Williams, and this is my sister, Kathy. We live over there by the road. Would you like to come home and have a cup of tea or something? That was a bad fall you took. You must be shaken up."

The ton weight slowly disappeared and I could breathe again, but I still felt as though I had been run over by a freight train. "Thanks," I said, "but I'm okay, really. I'm

Joanna Longfellow, by the way. I ride for Holmwood Farms. I have to get on Othello again and ride him back. That's a must when you fall off." I was grateful for their concern, but I couldn't help adding, "I knew he was going for the tree, but he has a hard mouth and I couldn't turn him in time. I'm used to show-jumping in the ring, and this was the first time I've ridden him. He's been penned up for weeks, and he was excited."

I saw the astonishment mingled with respect on their faces when I mentioned Holmwood Farms. I tried to stand up, and a searing pain ran down my back and through my leg. I must have turned white because Dinah said, "You can't ride him back until you've had a rest anyway. You'd better come home with us. Kathy can lead the horse back, and I'll help you."

I had had pulled muscles and sprains before in my short riding career, but this was the worst yet. I had no doubt that a spot of heat applied to the sprain and a short rest would set me up again, but meanwhile I was through with being brave; it hurt too much. I draped my arm round Dinah's slight shoulders, and together we managed a slow hobble. Kathy approached Othello gingerly, looking very small beside his bulk, but he let her take the dangling reins and followed her like a lamb, although I noticed she kept looking back over her shoulder as though not quite trusting him. We followed a trail through the seedling trees and through a gate to the road. I saw the gray stone cottage opposite, and immediately it dawned on me that these must be the children of Mrs. Williams—the Mrs. Williams who, with the cooperation of my father, had successfully conspired to blight my life. Instinctively I recoiled and withdrew my arm from Dinah's shoulder.

"What's the matter?" she asked, puzzled.

It wasn't fair to take it out on them, but I couldn't help myself. "I'm supposed to be having lessons with your mother. That's what's the matter," I said. "My parents arranged it without consulting me, and because of it I'm going to lose my Saturday-morning job. I'm kind of furious about it, and I don't think I particularly want to meet your mother right now."

Dinah looked at me and said hesitantly, "Oh, you must be the girl who failed in English. Mother told us." She shrugged her shoulders in a helpless gesture. "Well, I'm sorry, but we didn't know, and we needed the money—and anyway if it hadn't been my mother, it would probably have been someone else."

Kathy had come up with Othello and stood beside her sister, the two of them overshadowed by the big horse. There was something rather defiant and pathetic about them, as though they felt obliged to stand up for their mother against me when it was not in their nature to be belligerent. It was I who was supposed to feel wronged, but they were making me feel like the villain of the piece. Anyway, Dinah was right. If it hadn't been her mother, it would probably have been someone else, and I didn't see what choice I had but to accept their hospitality since I could hardly stand for the pain in my back and leg.

"Oh, all right," I said, none too graciously. "Let's go."

We took up our weird procession again, me hobbling and leaning on Dinah, and Kathy leading Othello as though she were treading on eggshells. He was being extremely docile and passive now he had had his fun, and the only worry I had about him was how I was going to get him back to his paddock before he was missed.

As we went up the path to the front door of the cottage, it opened, and a woman came out on to the step and stared at us as though she didn't quite believe what she saw. At first I didn't think she could be Mrs. Williams because she was so unlike Dinah and Kathy, who were both very slight and somewhat mousey—she was buxom and dark-haired with a real peaches-and-cream complexion. But she said, "What on earth . . . ?" and Dinah said, "Mother, this is Joanna Longfellow from Holmwood Farms."

Mrs. Williams came down the steps and looked at me; at least I thought she was looking at me, but then I realized that she had eyes only for Othello. She went right past me, took his reins from Kathy, and said with shining eyes, "What a gorgeous horse!" She stroked his head and scratched his neck, and if ever there was love at first sight, this was it. "Where on earth did you find him?" she asked. "He's beautiful!"

"Mother," said Dinah pointedly. "This is Joanna Longfellow. He's her horse. She fell off him. She's hurt."

I honestly don't believe she had noticed me before, but now she was full of concern as she saw the sorry plight I was in. "Oh, you poor child!" she cried, making up for her momentary lapse. "Here, let me help you." She took over from Dinah and had me settled in the house in no time, checking me over for suspected fractures, putting my feet up, giving me a heating pad for my back, and putting the kettle on to make me a cup of tea. She was efficient and reassuringly hearty. It was easy to see that she had been a schoolteacher. I couldn't help liking her, even though I tried not to.

Meanwhile, Dinah was bringing her mother up to date, explaining what had happened and who I was, including the fact that I was to be her new pupil, but tactfully omitting to repeat my feelings on the matter. We had all forgotten poor Kathy standing outside with Othello until she put her head in the door and asked plaintively, "Mother, what am I supposed to do with this horse?"

She sounded so tragic, we all had to laugh, and Mrs. Williams left Dinah to finish making the tea while she found somewhere to tie up Othello securely.

It was a cozy little room, small but with some good pieces of furniture in it, and the curtains and slipcovers were bright and cheerful. I found I was actually enjoying being pampered. Nobody ever pampered me at home. Mrs. Williams had given me some aspirin, and with my feet up and a couple of cushions and the heating pad behind my back, the pain had become bearable. If I could stay here for an hour or so, I felt sure I would be so much better I would be able to ride Othello back before anyone missed him at feeding time. As usual, I was already beginning to regret my impulsive behavior now the fuel of my anger had burned down to a spark.

Mrs. Williams came back into the house, and she had that starry-eyed look about her again. "He's so beautiful," she said. "Such a big softie. I used to ride a horse like him when I was a girl. That was ages ago, of course." She sighed, then laughed at herself for being sentimental. "Are you feeling better?" she asked me. "Do you think you're going to be able to ride him back, or should I call somebody to come and get you."

That was the last thing I wanted. I told her hastily that I would be just fine if I could rest for a little while, and she said that was okay with her, and meanwhile she would go over to the neighboring farm to see if she could rustle up some oats for Othello in case he was hungry after his mad ride. If she wanted to make up to Othello, that suited me fine so long as it gave me time to recover. Kathy and Dinah stayed behind and pumped me about my riding. Holmwood Farms happens to be a very impressive place, and the house sitting by itself on top of the hill is an architectural showpiece. They seemed quite awed when I told them that John Holmes was my boyfriend, although I wasn't seeing too much of him at the present moment.

"Not that I ever did," I told them, "except on weekends and holidays. The family has a stockbroking business in Toronto, and they have an apartment there. John's grandfather retired a couple of months ago and lived in the house for a while, but now he's gone to stay with his daughter in Florida, and John's mother died when he was very young. There's only the housekeeper living there during the week. Mr. Holmes comes up every weekend and takes over my training from Jim Stiles, who's in charge of the stables. Usually John would have been home now for the summer vacation, but he's gone on a canoe trip to James Bay with some friends, and he won't be back until August."

I had been quite unhappy when John had told me about

the trip, but as he had pointed out, it wasn't much fun sitting at home doing nothing while I spent all my time training for the Royal. Reluctantly I had had to agree with him. At least he wasn't likely to meet too many stunning girls, plodding through the northern Ontario bush, being bitten half to death by blackflies and mosquitoes.

When Kathy and Dinah had learned everything there was to know about me, they told me about themselves. Dinah was twelve and Kathy ten. They had come to Toronto from England two years ago and had moved into the stone cottage only last month, so they hadn't been to school yet and didn't know anybody. I still couldn't get over how unlike their mother they looked.

"You two must look like your dad," I said.

There was a moment's pause before Dinah said, almost too quickly, "Yes—yes, I guess we do."

Noticing nothing, putting my big foot in it as usual, I went merrily on. "Does he work near here? My father writes for a television studio in Toronto, and he's away quite a bit"—but not often enough, I added to myself sourly, remembering how I had got myself into this scrape in the first place. Still, things hadn't turned out too badly. I liked these two girls with their earnest little pixy faces, and I even liked their pretty mother, whom I had been prepared to hate with all my heart. Thinking they looked a bit despondent, I said cheerfully in my best girl-scout manner, "I bet you'll like it better here than Toronto when you get used to it. I wouldn't go back to the city for anything."

Something had gone wrong. Kathy was scowling at me, her fine brows drawn together in a straight line. "Our father is away," she said fiercely.

"Oh, Kathy!" Dinah sighed and clasped her hands together uncomfortably. "He is not away, and you know it."

"He is! He is! He's away!"

Dinah jumped up and faced her sister squarely. Her face was screwed up in some kind of private agony. "He's divorced, Kathy! He's divorced! Why won't you say it? He's not away. He and Mother are divorced. People have to know sooner or later. It's not a disgrace. Why won't you say it?"

Kathy stood up, too, her cheeks scarlet. She had forgotten me. "He's away!" she hissed at Dinah. "He's away!" She turned and pushed from the room, slamming the door behind her.

I felt terrible, as though I were an unwanted intruder. I stood up, feeling that Dinah would want me to leave, but the pain shot through my back the moment I got to my feet, and I had to sit down again.

Dinah looked at me unhappily. "Don't mind Kathy," she said with a sigh. "She won't accept it—that's all. But she will one day. It's just too new at the moment for her to accept."

She looked so woebegone standing there, nervously fumbling with the buttons on her sweater, that I forgot my own troubles. "You don't have to talk about it," I said. "Unless you want to, that is."

"I don't mind," she said philosophically. "Lots of parents get divorced. It's not so terrible when you get used to it. I guess it's worst of all for Mother. You see, everything was going to be so good; then it went wrong. Daddy had his own business in London, but we always wanted to live on a farm because Mother had been brought up on one.

Then we finally did get a farm in Cornwall, and Kathy and I had ponies, and it was lovely. But Daddy's business went bankrupt, and we would have lost the farm except that a friend offered him a job in Canada. So he came over here, and he was going to send for us if he liked it, or else make enough money to start again in England." Her voice faltered. I hoped she wasn't going to cry, but she took a deep breath and took a hold on herself. "Anyway, he didn't send for us. He kept putting us off until Mother decided to sell the farm and come over anyway—and then she found that there was somebody else—" She shrugged her shoulders and gave a brave little laugh. "So here we are. We lived in Toronto for a while, but Mother didn't like the city so we decided to try living in the country. Mother has a part-time job in the library, so I guess it's going to be all right." She looked apologetic for burdening me with her troubles, but I think she was glad to talk about it to someone outside her own family.

As for me, I was suddenly realizing that a lot of people were a great deal worse off than I was. I was ashamed and wanted very much to do something for Dinah and Kathy. "You'll have to come around and visit us," I said eagerly. "I'll show you over Holmwood Farms if you want. We only live next door. We have two horses of our own, as well—at least Horse belongs to Grandma, but Horse the Second is ours. You'll love him."

I explained to her how Mr. Archer had always called his horses Horse, because he couldn't remember names, and very soon I had her laughing. We talked about school for a while and about my family, and since it was a time for confessions, I told her how I had sneaked out with Othello because I was furious with my father, and if anyone found out what I had done, I would be in more hot water. It seemed to do her good to hear that I had troubles, too, and we were getting along famously when Mrs. Williams came in with Kathy. They had been feeding Othello oats, and Kathy seemed quite all right again. I knew I had to leave soon, or I would never get Othello home before he was missed.

"I really must go now," I said. "Thank you so much for being so kind and everything." But the minute I stood up, there was the pain again as bad as ever. I couldn't hide it from them, and Mrs. Williams looked very concerned. "I think I'd better ring up your parents," she said. "You can't ride back. That's out of the question."

"No, don't do that!" I could just imagine how happy my father would be to learn that I had taken a horse from Holmwood Farms without permission. He and Mr. Holmes had become good friends since we had moved next door, but one of my father's most important rules was that you didn't take advantage of friendship and you respected other people's property.

"Why don't you tell my mother?" Dinah urged me. "She'll understand."

I really didn't have any alternative, and anyway she had it out of me in no time flat. She must have been an excellent schoolteacher in her day.

"So," she said when I had confessed all, and there was a trace of a smile playing about her lips, "it looks as if I'm the bogeyman that's caused all the trouble. Oh, dear!

But you can't stay here, Joanna. Someone's going to miss you and Othello sooner or later."

I set my thought processes working furiously. "If only I could get Othello back without anyone noticing," I said desperately. "My family are used to me limping and hobbling around, so they'd only think I hurt myself jumping Queenie in the ring. But how can I get Othello back?"

"Can't you ride him back, Mother?" asked Dinah.

"Me!" She looked horrified. "Dinah, I haven't ridden for over twenty years! I wish I could, but if he runs away with Joanna, what would be do with me? Anyway I still wouldn't have any idea where to put him when I got him there. I don't want to be pinched for trying to steal a horse."

Maybe it was the mention of crime, but I suddenly thought of my brothers. They thrived on conspiracy, and if only I could get them alone and explain to them, I knew they would throw themselves heart and soul into the business of getting Othello back unseen.

I looked at Mrs. Williams timidly, uncertain as to how she would react. "I wonder—do you think you could possibly drive me to the gate of my house and drop me off?" I explained that if I could get Maxwell and Julian alone I was sure they would help me, but nobody must see me getting out of Mrs. Williams' car or there might be awkward questions asked.

Kathy clapped her hands, delighted at all this scheming against adults. "Oh, Mother, do take her, please!"

"Yes, do, Mother," pleaded Dinah. "After all, you did ruin Joanna's job for her, so you do owe her something."

Mrs. Williams gave in because she was outnumbered, and I think she had something rather girlish about her, too, behind her capable manner. "On one condition," she said, "that you have your back seen to. I don't care how you explain it to your parents, but I think you ought to have it looked after."

I promised that I would. I wasn't too keen to go around in this crippled state, either, particularly with the intensified training Mr. Holmes had set up for me.

It wasn't very far to our house, but on the way over, Mrs. Williams said thoughtfully without taking her eyes from the road, "You know, Joanna, I hate the thought of your losing your job because of me. I told your father Saturday mornings would be most convenient for me, because I work in the mornings during the week and I like to catch up on my housework in the afternoons. However, in your case, I think I could make an exception. How about Monday afternoons instead?"

I could have kissed her, if my back hadn't hurt so much. Instead we smiled at each other, and I knew I wasn't going to mind having lessons with her at all—not even during vacation. In fact, I felt so good and loving toward everybody, I was even ready to go home and forgive my father.

Jim Plays Detective

I FOUND Maxwell and Julian sitting on the fence, watching Horse the Second run rings around his mom. Our three dogs were sprawled at their feet. We had always wanted pets, but before we moved to the country all we could have was hamsters. Now everyone unloaded their strays on to us, until Father threatened to call the house Pound Farm. There was Seal, who was small, sleek, and wet-looking; big, square Jumbo; and Horsefeathers, a homemade, knitted type of dog, who looked exactly the same fore and aft. Their chorus of welcoming barks alerted my brothers as I hobbled toward them. They looked me over with clinical appraisal.

"What's she done now, d'you suppose?" asked Julian.

"I don't know," commented Maxwell. "Broken another leg, I expect."

I resisted an impulse to clink their heads together and

told them I needed their help. They listened without turning a hair.

"It'll cost you," said Julian.

"No, it won't," I told him, "or I'll tell Father how the well cover happened to end up in the duck pond."

Maxwell raised his brows, all innocence. "How *did* the well cover end up in the duck pond?"

"You know very well how it did. You were reading that article on how to build a sailboat out of concrete, and you thought you'd experiment with a raft. Only it didn't work, did it?"

"We'll go," said Maxwell hastily.

"Right," I said, "and leave the dogs behind because you look like a circus. And don't try and ride Othello back, or we'll all end up cripples. And don't let anybody see you putting him in his paddock."

The last I was almost yelling because they were already on their bicycles pedaling down the driveway. I wasn't particularly worried anymore because, in spite of their being so obnoxious, I had quite a lot of faith in my brothers. The dogs were very obedient. They had been told to stay, and they stayed, but they looked quite disconsolate about it. I patted their heads and limped into the house. I had seen Grandma's vintage model car outside, so I knew she was visiting Mother. I found them having coffee in the kitchen. Father had taken himself off somewhere. He couldn't stand Grandma's comments on what she would have been doing to her house if she were him. Simultaneously they put down their coffee mugs and rose from their chairs, as I flopped into the nearest one I could find.

"What happened to you?" they exclaimed.

I didn't like telling lies, but I had learned from Maxwell and Julian the fine art of bending and wiggling the truth to suit the occasion. "I was riding, and I fell off," I said.

"You didn't tell us you were going to have a lesson today," said Mother.

I shrugged, which could have meant anything, and she started fussing around, getting me to stand up and bend over, and go into contortions to see in which position I squealed most. "I think we ought to take her to the doctor," she said to Grandma. "Jim didn't let you walk back, did he, Joanna?"

"Nope," I said, giving my best impression of Hamilton Schumacher.

"Well, I should hope not. Sometimes I think he's pushing you too hard. How high did you jump today?"

I did a quick mental calculation of the height of the fence I had jumped on Othello and said, "About four feet."

"I don't know why you have to jump at all," said Grandma. "In my day girls were quite satisfied to go for a ladylike canter."

In her day they had probably ridden sidesaddle, too, and worn long riding habits, and fainted every five minutes because their corsets were too tight, but I didn't feel like getting into an argument. I thought that my back would probably get better by itself, but Mother insisted I go to the doctor. Father had taken our car, so Grandma drove us in hers. It's a good thing I wasn't an emergency, or I would have been dead long before we reached the village. If

Grandma drove more than twenty-five miles an hour, she thought she was being very daring and reckless, and kept cocking her ear for sirens.

The doctor put me on a table, prodded and punched me, and announced that I probably had a pinched nerve, that I should go to bed and do absolutely nothing, and if it wasn't better in a few days, I should have some X rays. The decision didn't distress me as much as it would have ordinarily. There is nothing like being an invalid for having people forget your shortcomings, and luckily I didn't have any immediate shows coming up. In fact, I thought it would be rather fun to have everyone running around at my beck and call for a while, particularly Father. I hoped he would be sorry now for the way he had treated me.

Mother and Grandma were already treating me like fragile china as they helped me back into the car and bundled me up in rugs. "It's a good thing it wasn't next week," said Mother. "Then you would have missed your first lesson with Mrs. Williams, and that would have been a poor beginning."

I didn't think this was the time to tell her I had changed my lessons to Monday afternoons, because I couldn't think of a way to explain my meeting with Mrs. Williams, but I had plenty of time now to dream up something. When I was up and about again, I could always go to the library, and my parents would think I had met her there and made other arrangements. Jim would have to be told, too, because I wouldn't be able to have my lessons over the weekend when Mr. Holmes came up from the city, but that didn't present much of a problem. Maxwell and

Julian were always hanging around Holmwood Farms, and they could tell him I'd pulled a muscle in my back without going into details. As far as he was concerned, it could have happened any time, and no one need be any the wiser.

So, with everything worked out in my mind to my satisfaction, I mentally crossed my fingers, and allowed myself to be put to bed, trying to look as pathetic and wan as possible to arouse everyone's sympathy.

Maxwell and Julian were my first visitors. They looked smug and very pleased with themselves.

"Everything went off without a hitch," Julian assured me. "We walked Othello back and sneaked him into his paddock. If anybody saw us, we were going to say we were exercising him, but nobody did. Jim was out with the truck, and the others were in the barn getting the feed ready. That Mrs. Williams is nice, and so are her kids except that they're girls."

"Male chauvinist pig," I said.

"You'd better be careful what you say to us," warned Maxwell, "because we know too much."

"I know some things about you, too," I reminded him, "and I want you to do something else for me. I want you to go over and see Jim before Mother and Dad start gabbing to him. Tell him I won't be riding for a week because an old back injury's acting up."

Maxwell made a mental note of this. "You want us to tell him you injured your old back?"

"Don't be smart!" I hissed at him. Sometimes they exasperated me beyond words. "Tell him it's not serious, but I think I should lay off the lessons for a week, so I'll be perfectly fit for the next show. You know the sort of thing—don't make him worried; that's all. I don't want him asking too many questions."

"What if it's not better by next week?" asked Julian cheerfully.

I hadn't even considered such a prospect. "Of course it will be!" I said impatiently. "The doctor says it's a pinched nerve, and all it takes is rest. I can't stand your sort. You're the kind of person who goes to visit someone in hospital and tells them how many people you know who've died lately. Are you going to see Jim or not?"

"I can't stand tyrant invalids," sniffed Julian. "I'd rather be a male chauvinist pig than an invalid tyrant any day."

They shuffled out, muttering to themselves, and were soon replaced by Margaret who stuck her head round the door and said cheerily, "Goofing off again, I see. I don't know how you get away with it."

"A person would have to be dead for six weeks around here," I said, disgruntled, "before they got any sympathy. Did you know your boyfriend leaks?"

"What do you mean—leaks?" she said, incensed.

"His stuffing's coming out. A seam must have split. I shoveled up two bags of grain from the kitchen yesterday after he left."

"Oh—you!" she spluttered, banging the bedroom door and clumping down the stairs. I wasn't having much luck in the sympathy line except for Seal, Jumbo, and Horsefeathers, who were so sorry for me they were lying all over my bed, squashing me.

Father came up eventually and shooed them all out. He said awkwardly, "How are you feeling, chicken?" I knew he was feeling bad about bawling me out earlier, but didn't like to admit it.

"I'm fine," I said in a wan voice, "except for this agonizing pain every time I breathe, and these awful cramps in my legs and arms."

He looked alarmed. "Maybe I'd better get your mother."

"Oh, no, I'm all right," I assured him with a brave sigh. "You get used to it in time."

"Well," he said, looking down at me and scratching his beard thoughtfully, "I hope you are going to be better by next week because I've sent Mrs. Williams a check in advance for your lessons. I don't know why you can't time things better, Joanna. You don't seem to have any sense of coordination."

Neither did I have any words at that moment, I was so disgusted with my family. Only the delicious supper Mother prepared especially for me restored my spirits to something slightly below normal. The doctor had given me some painkillers, and I dozed off early, waking briefly as Maxwell and Julian thundered through my sickroom to the sleeping porch on their way to bed.

"Did you see Jim?" I asked them in a dopey voice.

Julian gave me the thumbs-up sign. "Everything's okay. He said if you've hurt your back you'd better rest it, and one week off won't hurt your riding. It might even do it good."

I smiled to myself as I dropped back to sleep, feeling better about everything. My family couldn't help their unfortunate natures, and Maxwell and Julian were really little treasures after all.

Next morning I awoke to bright sunlight streaming through the window. It was rather pleasant to listen to everyone going about their business and to know that I didn't have to do anything at all. Blob, the cat, was already sleeping on my bed, and soon Jumbo nosed the door open and joined him, followed by Seal and Horsefeathers. I felt like Noah stranded on Mount Ararat, and was glad that Horse and Horse the Second didn't have access to the house. Mother came up with my breakfast and ordered Maxwell and Julian to clear my room of animals. She brought me some magazines and books, and I had my transistor radio. Altogether, I thought, this wasn't a bad life, not for a few days anyway. I should have known better. After lunch Jim came to see me.

He was the last person I had expected, knowing that this was the busy time at Holmwood Farms, with the haying in full swing, and several two-year-olds in the process of being broken. Mother showed him up to my room and went back to her housework. He sat down beside my bed and looked me over with a wry smile on his face. He had a lean, leathery face, with the brightest blue eyes I had ever seen. It was hard to have secrets from Jim.

"So, sweetheart," he said, with his tongue in his cheek, "you were jumping Queenie yesterday, and you had a fall, eh?"

I went red in the face and spluttered. "Who told you that?"

"Your mother. We were having a little chat downstairs. She thought maybe I was pushing you too hard."

I squirmed under the covers. "What did you tell her?"

"I didn't tell her anything. All I know is what your brothers told me. I was passing by so I thought I'd drop in and see how you were. Now I hear from your mother that we had a lesson yesterday, that you jumped four feet on Queenie, fell off, and hurt your back. She also thanked me for driving you home."

I couldn't meet the quizzical look on his face. I felt like pulling the sheets over my head. "She—she's got it all wrong," I stuttered.

"You'd better believe it, sweetheart. Were you riding Queenie, yesterday?"

Like a cornered animal, I started hedging. "You said I could ride Queenie anytime in the arena, so long as I didn't do anything stupid. You said the more I rode her the better. You said you trusted me."

"I *did* trust you, Joanna."

I didn't like the emphasis he put on that word at all. "What do you mean?" I asked nervously.

His blue eyes bored right into me. "You weren't riding Queenie yesterday, Joanna, because the blacksmith was here in the afternoon, trimming her hoofs."

Oh, boy, I thought, now I have to get out of this one! Countering desperately, I said, "Well, I didn't say I actually rode Queenie. There are other horses I exercise—you know that. You said a good rider shouldn't stick with one horse. I thought you liked me to exercise some of the others for a change."

"In the arena, yes."

"Well?" I said defiantly, feeling I didn't have anything more now to lose—but I had.

Jim looked at me sadly, shaking his head. "No one rode in the arena yesterday, Joanna. The fellows were putting fresh sawdust down and had the hoses on. Suppose you forget all that double-talk and tell me the truth. You were riding Othello, weren't you?"

How could he have known? I could only think that Maxwell and Julian must have let something out by mistake. For all their faults, I knew they wouldn't have done it purposely. Still, riding Othello in his paddock was not such a dreadful offence. I tried to brazen it out, getting myself more and more tied up in knots, until Jim lifted his hand impatiently. "Come on, Joanna, don't give me any of that! You took Othello out—a horse you'd never ridden, that you knew nothing about—and he ran away with you and threw you. Isn't that what happened?"

"How did you know?" I whispered tremulously.

"Because he had burs in his tail, sweetheart, and you don't get burs in a bare paddock, so I just put two and two together. Now why would you do a thing like that? That's what I want to know."

I gave up. He was too smart for me. With the tears streaming down my face, I confessed everything—how my father had made me so mad, and how I was going to lose my job, and all I had wanted to do was ride fiercely to get rid of my frustration. "But I didn't take Queenie!" I cried out, trying to exonerate myself. "I was going to, but I didn't, so I'm not so bad! I did have second thoughts about that. I realized she was valuable, and it would be a reckless, silly thing to do, so I took Othello."

Jim's eyebrows shot up. "You mean his life isn't

valuable? You didn't know a thing about him, whether you could control him or not. Suppose he'd run out onto the highway and hit a car. You could have been killed, and so would he have been, and you could have caused a terrible accident. And what if he'd stumbled down a groundhog hole and broken a leg? The end of a fine, healthy horse, but I suppose that doesn't matter because Joanna says he isn't valuable. Do you value life in terms of dollars then? Oh, Joanna, sometimes I despair of you."

I couldn't bear him saying that. "I'm sorry!" I wailed through my tears. "I really am! I was so mad, I just didn't think. Please don't tell Mr. Holmes, Jim! Please don't!"

Jim sighed heavily. He had his cap in his hands. He stood up and stuck it on the back of his head, looking down at me in my misery. "I won't tell Mr. Holmes, Joanna," he said wearily, "but sometimes I despair of ever making a championship rider out of you."

"But I'm good!" I cried, my pride stung. "I've won seven red ribbons in three months!"

Jim gave me a sad smile. "That's small stuff you're doing now, Joanna. I'm not knocking it, because it's a start and you've mastered the technique of riding better than anyone I know in such a short time. But until you mature and get your emotions under control, you're never going to get up there into the championship class because you have no discipline at all." He waved down my objection impatiently. "Oh, you've got plenty of discipline when it comes to practicing—I'll grant you that. In fact you're a holy terror for work. But a champion has to discipline his emotions as well. He doesn't go off half-cocked at every little upset in his life. You're hopelessly immature, Joanna. I can't help wondering if you're ever going to grow up."

I was humiliated to my very bones. Here I had been playing the big shot, giving myself fancy airs to impress Dinah and Kathy, and now I felt less than nothing, my pride in shreds. Even Jim had to feel sorry for my abject state. He came back to the bed and ruffled my hair.

"All right, sweetheart. I've said my piece, and that's it. There's always tomorrow. I hope you got a good scare. We won't mention this to anyone else. Now hurry up and get better. Remember there's the Junior Grand Prix coming up in four weeks."

I couldn't believe I was being given another chance. "Oh, Jim," I said gratefully, "I'll be so good in the future you won't know me. I promise! Oh, I promise!"

The twinkle came back into his eyes. "Now don't go jumping overboard again. You can start by doing exactly as the doctor says, right?"

"Right," I echoed happily. Still there was something I felt I had to set him right on. "Jim—"

"What, sweetheart?"

"I didn't fall off Othello. I wasn't scared of him at all. He ran under a tree, and a branch knocked me off—that's all."

"Oh, so that's all, is it?" He tried to appear stern, but he couldn't make it. When he went out of the room, he was laughing to himself. As for me, I felt I had been reprieved from the death sentence. Then and there I made a vow to myself: I would change; I would strive henceforth to be rational, clear-thinking, steady and reliable, equal to cope with any emergency. I was half in love with the idea of this new Joanna Longfellow already and couldn't wait to begin playing her. Of one thing I was certain—I was never again going to give anyone cause to call me immature.

The End of My World

I HAD been in bed three days, and I had been so patient, kind, and sweet that Maxwell and Julian were begining to find me nauseating.

"Are you sure you didn't fall on your head?" asked Maxwell suspiciously, as they passed through my room in their swimming trunks ready for an afternoon of fun at the Holmes's swimming pool.

"Why do you say that, Maxwell?" I said, smiling at him benevolently.

"Because you're getting to be a pain in the neck, that's why. You never answer back or anything." He leaned forward confidentially. "You want to know something? Mother and Dad think you're not long for this world."

"Oh, Maxwell," I said with a tinkling laugh. "You bad boy. You do tell fibs. I hope you two have a lovely afternoon swimming. Come back and tell me all about it, won't you?"

"Yuck!" Maxwell looked as though he were about to throw up. "Let's get out of here. It might be catching."

As Julian came thudding past, he stopped to give me a huge wink. "You can't fool me. I know you're up to something. Have you got a boyfriend hidden in the closet?"

For a moment I almost lost my cool, but a deep breath saved me. By the time I had let it out, they were gone. I was really pleased with the new me. I felt sure my new tranquility had to be reflected in my riding. I was so calm and in control of myself that I wasn't even scared at the thought of the Junior Grand Prix, which would be the stiffest course I had yet done, coming up at the beginning of August. There was a $250 first prize, the first time I had competed for money, and already I had spent it, not on myself as the old Joanna would have done, but on gifts for my family. Even my face looked different, I thought, studying myself in the mirror opposite my bed, sort of ethereal and pure, with a touch of sadness about the eyes which, I thought, was rather interesting. I could hardly wait for John to come home to find that his Funny Face had grown up into a mature, intelligent woman.

Next day I had to go back to the doctor for his verdict. I was disappointed to find my back still ached, and in certain positions the pain was still there, but not quite so bad. I told the doctor that it was only natural since I was stiff as a board from lying in bed, but as soon as I got back to riding again, I would limber up and be fine. He thanked me for my diagnosis, but thought he should take some X rays anyway, just to be on the safe side.

"Very well, Doctor," I said, smiling at my mother, who had expected me to blow my top. "Anything you say, but I would be obliged if you would let me know the results soon, because I have an important show coming up at the end of the month, and since I'm entering the Royal in November, I really can't waste much more time lying in bed."

He promised me he would let my parents know by tomorrow, but meanwhile I could get up and go downstairs, so long as I didn't do anything strenuous. This seemed like a good omen to me, and I was very happy going home in the car. But instead of bubbling all over the way I would have done before, I remembered to control my emotions as Jim had said, and just smiled serenely to myself. Mother was driving our car this time because Father was at home, working on a script.

"Are you sure you feel all right, Joanna?" she asked me. "You're so quiet."

"Yes, Mother," I replied demurely. "I feel marvelous."

She looked as though she didn't believe me. In fact she kept looking at me all the way home, until she nearly ran into a bus and was forced to keep her eyes on the road.

It was nice to be downstairs again. I could watch television, and I even dried the dishes. Margaret brought Hamilton Schumacher to supper, and all through the meal I made a point of studying him to try and find his good points. In the end I discovered two: he had nice teeth, and since he never said anything, he could never bore anyone to death. I felt very pleased about this because I had been almost sure he had no fine points at all.

"Good night, Hamilton," I said, when he left with Margaret to go to a movie. "I hope to see you again soon."

He looked at me in astonishment, his eyes nearly popping out of his baby face, and I felt I had taken a big stride in the right direction.

But, alas, for my good intentions! Mother and Father had to go into Kitchener next day to do some shopping, and they promised to call in at the doctor's office on their way back to find out when I could start riding again. Meanwhile, I was supposed to have a rest in bed after lunch, and because I was still taking some kind of a pill that made me dopey, I fell into a nice restful sleep, dreaming about the day soon to come when I could be reunited with Queenie. I awoke in a pleasant stupor to see my mother and father standing at the foot of my bed, watching me in silence. The bedroom door was shut, but as I tried to clear my fuzzy head of sleep, I saw it open a crack, and Maxwell, Julian, and Margaret peered in with dreadful solemn looks on their faces. There was none of the giggling and pushing that usually accompanied their eavesdropping. This alarmed me more than anything else. Mother and Father were looking at me so strangely, and yet they seemed unable to say anything. It was so quiet in the room, I could hear Horse calling to Horse the Second way across the field behind the barn.

"What is it?" I cried, sitting up. "What happened? Did someone die?"

For a dreadful moment I thought of Grandma and Mr. Archer, who after all were both old people, even if they did seem in the best of health.

Mother assured me hastily. "No, dear, no. It's nothing like that."

"Then what is it?"

Mother turned to Father with a helpless gesture. "You tell her," she said. "I can't."

He came and sat down at the head of my bed and took one of my hands in his. "Joanna, we have some bad news for you. But you're my girl, aren't you? You can take it?"

"What?" I fairly screamed at him, forgetting all about tranquility and calmness under duress. "What are you all staring at me for?"

"Your X rays came back. It's a little worse than the doctor thought at first, but you're going to be able to ride again, so you mustn't worry."

"Then what—why?" I struggled out from under the covers and looked at them beseechingly. "What's the problem then?"

My father lifted his hands and dropped them again in a despairing sort of a gesture, and even in my bewilderment, I remember thinking that I had never seen him look so helpless before. Everything seemed to be unfolding in slow motion. I heard him say, "You did something to your spine when you fell, Joanna. It's the sort of thing that takes months to heal properly, and that means no riding—otherwise you may permanently injure your back. I'm afraid you're going to be grounded for a while."

I stared at him horrified. I felt icy trickles running through me. "How—how long?"

"That depends on how easy you take it. The doctor says six months to a year. You don't have to stay in bed, of course. You can lead a normal life as long as you don't do anything that might hurt your back again."

I couldn't believe him. I waited for them all to start jumping up and down gleefully, clapping their hands and yelling, "April fool!" except that it wasn't April, and nobody said anything. They just went on looking at me as if I were some sort of an exhibit on show. Then at last it sank in that this wasn't a joke. This was the real thing. "No!" I cried out. "You're lying! You're lying! It's not true."

"It's true, dear," said Mother. She was actually wringing her hands like the heroine in a late night B movie.

"But what about the Royal?" I cried. "That's only four months away." My voice rose to a squeal. "I'm riding Queenie in the Royal Horse Show, remember?" I felt that if I shouted loud enough, I could shout them down and make them change their verdict, tell me they were only fooling after all. But it didn't work. My father took me by the shoulders and turned my stricken face toward his.

"Joanna, you've got to face it. There won't be any Royal this year. These things happen. Injury is part of an athlete's life. It's something they have to learn to contend with. Are you listening to me?"

"No!" I cried, closing off my ears. "No!"

"There'll be other years, chicken. You're young yet. It's not the end of everything."

But for me it was. It was the end of my plans and dreams and hopes. For almost a year now I had thought of nothing but entering the Royal in November. Ever since John had gone to college and left his father without a rider, and Mr. Holmes had seen in me the raw material to take his place, it had been my one goal, my reason for living.

"But I want to do it this year!" I protested in vain. "I want to prove that I can, now, while I'm sixteen! I want to show Mr. Holmes and John and everybody that I can do it. Next year it won't be the same, and besides, if I don't ride all year, I won't be in any shape to go in next year either. And after that, I'll be too old!"

"Eighteen, Joanna?" said my mother, giving me a sad, whimsical little smile.

"Oh, you don't understand!" I cried, heartbroken. "You don't understand!" I turned to the wall and beat on it with my fists, wanting to destroy something in my terrible disappointment. "How can you ever understand!"

"We understand, Joanna. We understand how you feel, but you have to accept it, chicken. There's nothing else you can do."

My father tried to put his arm around me, but I shook him off. My anger turned on him. With blazing eyes I swung around and faced him. "How can you say you understand?" I accused him. "It was your fault! If you hadn't made me take lessons on Saturday mornings, it wouldn't have happened. Why didn't you understand then before it was too late? You didn't even bother to ask Mrs. Williams if she could take me any other time, when you knew it meant so much to me. You wanted me to lose my job to punish me—that's how much you understand!"

"Joanna, I don't know what you're talking about! That isn't true!"

"Isn't it? Then how come she says she can take me on a Monday—?"

I saw the query on their faces and realized, too late, that I had given myself away, but I no longer cared. Let my father feel bad. I wanted to make him feel responsible. I wanted to hurt someone as much as I had been hurt. I told them everything, and if I hadn't been feeling so terrible, I might even have enjoyed the shocked look on their faces. My father huffed and spluttered and didn't seem to know what to say.

"So it was your fault!" I flung at him, determined to rub it in. "If it hadn't been for you, I wouldn't have ridden Othello and fallen off. You're the one who's ruined my life. Now I hope you're satisfied!"

I pushed him aside and ran from the room. Margaret, Julian, and Maxwell stood aside almost reverently as I rushed by them and down the stairs. I really did think then that my life was over, that nothing would ever matter to me again. I even forgot the pain in my back as I ran across the yard toward the barn. I was past all thinking, feeling, or caring. The hurt inside me was greater than anything I had even known. I would have died cheerfully at that moment.

Horse and Horse the Second were out in the field. I crept like a wounded animal into their stall and flung myself on the ground, pulling the straw up and over me until I was buried. Then I cried and cried until some of the pain was gone, leaving behind a terrible bleak emptiness to take its place.

Nobody came after me. They must have known that this was something I must face alone, that they could do nothing for me until the worst of the hurt was over, and they respected my feelings. I don't know how long I lay there, covered in straw tickling my nose, and smelling the sweet scent of it all around me like a blanket. In the end I fell into a dark, tragic sleep, and later my father came down to the barn, picked me up like a baby, and carried me gently back to the house.

A New Start

I WENT through a bad time in the next couple of days. I couldn't accept that fate had dealt me this cruel blow just when things had seemed to be going so well. I lost faith in everything. I only wanted to stay in bed and see nobody. I ate the meals my mother brought me because it was easier than arguing, but I refused to talk to any of my family, and if they barged in anyway, I pulled the covers over my head. Mother told me that Jim would like to talk to me, but him, of all people, I couldn't face. I told her to send him away. The dogs still came into my bedroom, and sensing something wrong, whined for attention, but I was in such a terrible state of self-pity, I hadn't even time for them.

By the evening of the second day Father had had enough. After supper he came in, pulled the covers forcibly away from my head, and said, "Joanna, sit up. You and I are going to have a little talk."

I sat up woodenly, and fixed my gaze somewhere in the distance past his left shoulder. He was trying to be calm and patient, but I could hear his voice steaming up. "Joanna, this is enough of that nonsense. You've had a bad disappointment. We all appreciate that, and we've left you alone because we understand your feelings, but enough is enough. If this is the worst thing that happens to you in life, you'll be lucky. In two years at the most, you can have another go at the Royal. It's not as though you were crippled for life. It might even be a blessing in disguise because you've been neglecting your schoolwork shamefully. Now tomorrow you will get up and join the family again, if you still want to be a part of us. If you don't, well, you're sixteen, you can make other arrangements, but you're not going to stay here and make the rest of the family unhappy. Do I make myself clear?"

I couldn't believe anyone could be so callous as to say I was lucky, and he called himself understanding. I was seething inside, but it was better than the awful apathy that had possessed me for the last two days. Without looking at him, I said icily, "Yes, Father, you make yourself clear all right."

"Very good, then. Tomorrow morning I shall expect to see you at breakfast. Your mother has enough work to do without waiting on you like a slave."

He went out of the room, and I heard him going downstairs into the living room where the rest of the family were watching television. For a while I sat there thinking;

then I slipped out of bed and dressed. My father had said I could go, so I would go, exactly where I wasn't sure yet, but anywhere would be better than here, having to live with my unsympathetic family next door to Holmwood Farms where I would be reminded, every time I went out the door, of what I had lost. I took an overnight bag from the closet and packed a few necessities; then I sat down again on the bed and contemplated what I should do.

John had left home when he could no longer satisfy his father's overbearing ambition for him to become one of the top riders in the country, and he had made out all right. He had worked and got himself a scholarship to veterinary college, and his father had been so deeply hurt and shocked that he had become a changed man. Ambition had nearly lost him his only son, and trophies and ribbons became an empty substitute. Now he and John were reconciled, and they had never been happier. In training me to take John's place, Mr. Holmes had found a deeper satisfaction than perpetuating the glory of the family name. He had told me once that it didn't matter to him whether I entered competitions or not, so long as I fulfilled my desire to be a good rider, but unlike John, I had wanted to be the best, so we got along famously. Now that was over. Mr. Holmes would be distressed, but he had John again, and that was all that really mattered to him.

In my case it was different. My father had actually told me to go. He had made it clear that the family would be happier without me. Even in my anger I felt a lump in my throat at the thought. Well, if they didn't want me I wouldn't stay one moment longer. If John could make out all right, so could I. I should be able to find a job in Toronto easily enough because, whatever my father thought, I wasn't stupid.

Now I felt more rational about the whole thing. I would need some money for a start. I went down the landing to my parents' room and found my mother's purse. There was twenty dollars in it. I took it, but I didn't feel like a thief because of all those IOUs in the sleeping porch. Anyway, it would only be a loan. When I was making good money, I would return it with interest. When my preparations were complete, I put the money safely away in a pocket of my jeans, stowed the overnight bag away in the closet, and got back into bed, pulling the bedclothes up over my nose, so that no one would notice I was fully dressed. Soon Maxwell and Julian came through my room to bed, hardly bothering to give me a glance. If they had shown some concern for me, I might, even then, have changed my mind, but the novelty of my broken heart had already worn off, and they found me nothing but boring.

"All right," I said under my breath. "I hope you'll be sorry when you want someone to cover up for your crimes in future."

I waited a while longer, until Seal, Horsefeathers, and Jumbo one by one ambled through my room, pushing open the door to the sleeping porch where they spent the night. Even the dogs had lost interest in me. Now was the time to go, while Margaret and my parents were still watching television. I put on my jacket, took my bag, and crept down the stairs and out the front door.

The night was misty and melancholy, in keeping with the

way I felt. I kept my eyes straight ahead as I ran limping down the road. I didn't want to see the light of my own house receding in the distance, or the lanterns on top of the stone pillars at the gateway to Holmwood House. All that was finished and over, part of another Joanna in another life, as dead as I felt inside. It was nearly two miles to the stone cottage where Mrs. Williams lived. She had helped me once and I had liked and trusted her. There was nowhere else I could go to spend the night before I caught the early morning bus to Toronto. When my family woke up in the morning, I would be long gone.

I was glad to see a light in the window, which meant that Mrs. Williams was still up. When she opened the door to my ring, I stepped into the little hallway, put down my bag, and said, hoping I sounded as pathetic as I felt, "Please, may I stay here tonight? My father's told me to get out. I'll sleep on the floor if you like, and I'll be gone first thing in the morning, but I haven't anywhere else to go."

At first she just stared at me as though I were a ghost. She led me into the cozy room where I had been before, made me sit down and gave me a cup of hot chocolate. I must have looked cold and forlorn, although it was a warm enough night. She sat down opposite me and said I had better tell her what had happened. It was easier than I had feared it would be. After two days' silence I was bursting to talk to someone.

All the time she was watching me closely, and then she said, "Joanna, I can't believe your father turned you out of the house at this time of night. I've only talked to him once on the phone, but he seemed very nice and concerned about you."

"Well, he's not concerned any more," I said, scowling into my chocolate. "He actually told me the family would be better off without me, that I was sixteen now and I could leave—and that's the truth."

Mrs. Williams considered this for a moment. She looked skeptical. "I think I should have a talk with him," she said, standing up. "What's your phone number?"

I jumped up, too. "Oh, don't do that!" I begged her. "He'll be furious that I've come here!"

I should have known better than to come to a schoolteacher for refuge, even if she was an ex-schoolteacher. She wasn't going to take anything I said at face value. "I don't think you're telling me the whole story, are you, Joanna?" she said gravely. "I think you're running away from home and your parents don't know about it. Isn't that more like the truth?"

I tried to sidetrack her, but it was no use. Little by little she wrung the truth out of me, without any distortions. When she had finished, leaving me as limp as a rag, I noticed for the first time that Kathy and Dinah were standing in the doorway in their nightgowns, listening to every word. Mrs. Williams turned and saw them, too.

"What are you two doing here?" she said sharply. "Why aren't you in bed?"

"We just wondered who it was, Mother," said Dinah. "Is Joanna going to stay the night?"

Mrs. Williams looked a bit annoyed. "No, Dinah, I don't think so. Joanna's had a bit of trouble at home with her father, but everything's all right, so will you please go back to bed. You, too, Kathy."

I could tell that she was a firm mother, and used to being obeyed; nevertheless Kathy stood her ground and said with surprising intensity for such a delicate-looking child, "I wish my father was here! I wouldn't care whether he was mad at me or not, just so long as he was here. She's lucky to have a father!"

Mrs. Williams sighed heavily and went to the door. She said patiently, unhappily, as though she were repeating a lesson that had already been gone over several times, "Kathy, dear, you have a father, too, and he still cares about you. What's happened hasn't changed the way he feels about you one bit. Now will you please go to bed and get Dinah to tuck you in? I'll be in to kiss you good night presently."

Kathy went rebelliously, and Mrs. Williams turned back to me. For the first time I was beginning to feel a bit selfish, coming here and upsetting this little household that had troubles enough of its own. I felt suddenly very tired and unwanted. My back was beginning to act up again, and I didn't feel like coping with any more problems.

"Are you going to let me stay?" I asked miserably.

Mrs. Williams was regretful but firm. "No, Joanna. I'm sorry, dear, but I think you've had a row with your father, and you're acting on impulse. If you really want to leave home, you can do it properly with your parents' blessing, but this sneaking away in the middle of the night is just going to cause a lot of unnecessary unhappiness to everyone, yourself included. If you won't let me phone your parents, I think I should drive you home now, and you can talk it over with your mother in the morning."

It was a dreadful anticlimax, but I didn't really have any choice. It was either that, or ringing up my father to come and get me, and then the sparks would really fly.

"Do you have a key to your house?" asked Mrs. Williams. I nodded glumly, and she said, "In that case you can let yourself in, and no one need know anything about this. I won't say anything. When you've slept on it, I think you're going to feel quite differently in the morning."

I didn't, but what could I say? Mrs. Williams called out to Dinah and Kathy that she would only be gone a minute. Then she backed out her little car, and we drove home. I felt too down to say anything further, but as I was letting myself out of the car, Mrs. Williams leaned forward impulsively and touched my sleeve. "I hope you change your mind, Joanna. I was looking forward to coaching you. It would be nice to talk horses with someone again. It's years since I rode, but I miss it. I wouldn't leave all this if I were you. You don't know what a lucky girl you are."

That was the second time I had been called lucky tonight. I thought they must all be crazy, but I managed to squeeze out a halfhearted smile and thank her for her trouble. The house was in darkness, and she stayed outside the gate until I had let myself in, no doubt making sure that I didn't take off again. I didn't want to turn on the light in case I woke anyone up, and I nearly tripped over Blob, who had a nasty habit of twining himself around people's legs in the dark.

"Beat it, you miserable cat!" I hissed at him. I crept back up the stairs, feeling doomed to failure in whatever I undertook. There was a crack of light coming from underneath Margaret's door, and voices. Interested, in spite of myself, I stopped to listen. I wondered if she had had the nerve to sneak Hamilton Schumacher up to her room; I wouldn't put it past her. But as I pressed my ear to the door, I was startled to hear muffled sobs, and Mother's voice talking softly. Now I was really intrigued. I couldn't remember ever hearing Margaret cry before. She was aspiring to follow in Father's footsteps and become a writer, and as such she was given to suicidal fits of depression when first pages didn't turn out right, but this was something different.

I heard Mother's voice say gently, punctuated by Margaret's sniffles, "I know it's a sad thing to have happened, dear, but it's not the end of the world for Joanna. I know she thinks it is now, but life is full of disappointments and you have to learn to cope with them. You should know all about that. I remember two years ago when you were Joanna's age and had your first story rejected, you were ready to end it all, too. You survived and learned to accept rejection slips as part of the growing pains of becoming a good writer, and Joanna will survive, too. Don't worry."

Margaret blew her nose forcibly. "I know, but this is different. Joanna's absolutely lived for nothing else but the Royal Horse Show. Even when John was still at Holmwood Farms and Mr. Holmes hardly knew she existed, she used to dream about it. I hate seeing her like this, just lying there in bed, staring into space with that empty look in her eyes. I know she's a pain in the neck, but she is my sister, and I just wish there was something we could do to snap her out of it."

I was so stunned, I nearly fell through the door and gave myself away. Mother said, with a sigh that was clearly audible to me, "Don't you think we all wish that, Margaret? I know Daddy would willingly suffer for her if he could, but no one can do your growing up for you. There's nothing we can do, dear, except be patient and wait for time to do its own healing."

I didn't wait to hear any more. I crept back to my own room, feeling like a miserable worm. They did care about me, after all, even Father; and there was Margaret losing her beauty sleep over me while all I did was make fun of her boyfriends. It was incredible. If I hadn't heard it with my own ears, I wouldn't have believed it.

I sat on my bed in the darkness for a long, long time, thinking. Was it only a few days ago I had made a resolution to become mature? What a laugh that seemed now. I was a phony. I was arrogant, selfish, and spoiled, expecting the world to revolve around me. Maybe life was not as unplanned as it appeared to be, and had its own way of teaching people lessons. It was a bitter pill to swallow, but in the end I had to accept it. No one was to blame but me. No one had made me take Othello. I deserved everything that had happened to me.

I said it over and over again, pushing down the excuses that would keep popping up, even though it hurt to see myself as I really was. In the end, I got up and went back down the landing to Margaret's room. The light was out, and Mother had gone back to bed. I let myself in and stood in the darkness by the door, feeling suddenly self-conscious and foolish. Either Margaret had not been asleep, or the creaking of the door had woken her. The bedside light snapped on, and she sat up pale-faced and frightened, expecting an intruder. Seeing only me she flopped back on the pillows, expelling her breath in a windy gasp. "My God, Joanna, you scared me half to death! What are you doing?"

It wasn't how I had planned it at all. All my fine and noble thoughts of begging forgiveness evaporated, and left me tongue-tied. We were just not a sentimental family. I had wanted to tell her how touched I was to know that she cared about me, to tell her that in future I would bear my sorrow bravely and put my family before my broken heart because, in spite of everything, I truly loved them. But the words stuck in my throat, and all I could think of to say was, "I don't think Hamilton Schumacher's that bad, after all."

Margaret blinked her eyes and goggled at me. I think she wondered if she was still dreaming. She said incredulously, "You woke me up to tell me *that*!"

"Yes," I said. "That's all. Good night."

I turned to the door, feeling exceedingly uncomfortable and idiotic, when I was stopped by a strange sound. Turning suspiciously, I saw Margaret sitting up in bed trying to conceal her laughter by stuffing her closed fist into her mouth. Feeling hurt, I glared at her, but couldn't keep it up. Suddenly I was laughing, too, and we were giggling together helplessly.

"Oh, go back to bed. You're nuts!" she said at last impatiently. But I could tell she was much happier, and I was glad I had gone in to see her.

Next morning I went down to breakfast and everyone

treated me as though nothing unusual had happened at all. I was glad, because if anyone had mentioned the Royal or commiserated with me, I would have burst into tears and ruined all my good intentions.

I had made the first effort, and fate decided to give me a little reward. I was out on the verandah, watering the petunias in the flower boxes, when I happened to look up and see a handsome stranger standing in the yard. At least I thought it was a stranger, but when I looked closer, I saw that it was John, burned as brown as chocolate, his hair bleached to the color of pale straw. He was watching me with a little smile on his face. I threw down the hose which leaped around like a demented snake, soaking the three dogs who had latched on to me again now I had decided to rejoin the human race, and ran into his arms.

"Hi, Funny Face," he said, searching my eyes. "I just got back last night, and Jim told me. Do you want to talk about it?"

I pressed the tears back and gave him a wobbly smile. "No," I whispered. "Just hold me, John. It was bad for a while, but it's going to be all right now."

He cushioned my head on his shoulder, and we stood like that for a long time, each thinking our own thoughts and yet somehow knowing what the other was thinking. Then I took a deep breath and stood up straight, accepting things at last and feeling that in some strange unaccountable way I had taken my first real step toward maturity.

The Day of the Horse Show

NOW THAT John was home, I could bear up well enough, so long as I kept away from the stables and nobody talked to me about horses or shows. I couldn't avoid Mr. Holmes forever, of course, nor Jim, but John must have forewarned them because they were very tactful with me. They couldn't have been too happy about it, either. Both of them had spent a great deal of time on me, and had been counting on me to make a good showing for Holmwood Farms at the Royal, and now it would all come to nothing. I felt particularly guilty seeing Jim again, since he knew the truth of my escapade with Othello, and he had every right to be angry with me, yet all he said was, "Hurry up and get back into shape, sweetheart, because we're going to miss you around here." His kindness touched me so much I had to run out of the house and have my own quiet sniffle in Horse's barn. Horse didn't come into the category of other horses to be avoided because she was less like a horse than one of the family, and her back was a lovely broad place to bury my face in and have a private weep for all the things I had lost, while she contorted herself into a jackknife position to nibble at my pocket, looking for sugar lumps.

There was no reason now for me not to have my lessons on Saturday mornings with Mrs. Williams, since the doctor had said no heavy work or lifting, which meant I had lost my job at Holmwood Farms anyway, which was pretty ironical. Still, I couldn't be resentful. She was always so nice to me, and I used to stay to lunch with her and Dinah and Kathy, and I became very fond of them. If Mrs. Williams had hoped to talk horses, however, she was disappointed. That was one subject I avoided like the plague. Once she asked me if Othello had been sold yet. I told her I didn't know so abruptly that she got the message and never asked again.

So, mostly thanks to John, I survived the summer vacation, but there were funny times, too, like the time when Wallace Pindlebury arrived unexpectedly in his shocking-pink Volkswagen and informed us that he was going to stay for the week. He had been trying to sell his paintings on the Toronto sidewalks without success. "Man," he bewailed, "I'm years ahead of my time. Those cats just don't understand art when they see it."

Once we had had a standing feud, but now it was good to see his limp, lanky form draped over the kitchen table again, looking, as always, about to expire, with his straggly red hair in a ponytail and half a dozen good-luck charms strung around his neck. In his way, he seemed pleased to see me, too, and said that if I practiced transcendental meditation for eight hours every day and lived on bean sprouts and nuts, I could rise above my personal troubles and live in harmony and peace on cloud nine. I declined politely, but he was still sympathetic enough to add, "Well, like I mean, it's too bad. I mean, well, horses and you, man, that's real togetherness, if you know what I mean."

"Yes, Wallace," I sighed. "I know what you mean, though thousands wouldn't, but let's not talk about it, shall we, if you know what I mean?"

Margaret, meanwhile, was in a panic. Wallace didn't know about Hamilton Schumacher, and Hamilton Schumacher didn't know about Wallace. She didn't want to lose Hamilton, because Wallace would be going back to art college in a week, and she didn't want to tell Wallace about Hamilton because he believed that all his "cats" should be faithful to him, and him alone. "Like, man," he had told her once, "if you really care, you don't spread it around thin."

She cornered Maxwell, Julian, and me in the sun porch, and hissed urgently, "Get rid of Hamilton for a week. I don't care how you do it, but get rid of him, okay?"

"What's it worth?" asked Julian.

"Anything!" she answered recklessly. "Anything I've got!"

We mentally toted up that Margaret, who always had a boyfriend to squire her around and never had to spend any money of her own, must be worth at least twenty-five dollars from baby-sitting and other activities over the past year.

"Right," agreed Julian. "You're on."

We immediately went into a huddle and started conspiring. I threw out Maxwell's plan to kidnap Hamilton and hold him for ransom, thus lining our pockets as well as helping Margaret.

"It's got to be within the law," I said. "That's all I need now—to end up in jail for twenty years."

"Okay, let's tell him she's got smallpox, and the house is in quarantine for a week."

Julian was unimpressed. "He's probably been vaccinated, and besides, smallpox leaves scars on your face."

At this rate I could see we weren't going to get anywhere unless I took charge. At any moment Hamilton might finish work at the feed mill and come cycling up the road, leaving a trail of grain and happy birds behind him. Wallace with his transcendental meditation had given me an idea.

"We can say she's gone into retreat," I said, pleased at my brain wave. "We'll tell him she does it once a year to purify her mind, so it will be capable of producing great works, and anyone who doesn't respect her wish to be left totally alone during that period is a Philistine."

"What's a Philistine?" asked Maxwell suspiciously.

"I'm not quite sure," I said impatiently, "but it sounds good, and he won't know either, so let's get going."

I could manage to ride a bicycle for short distances, so we got out our bikes and cycled down to the feed mill in the village. Inside, it was noisy, dark, and cavernous, and smelled of molasses and dust. Hamilton was hefting sacks of grain in an innermost recess of the elevator. He was covered from head to foot in a soft white powder.

"Well," I said, "if it isn't Elmer, the friendly ghost. Greetings, Elmer. We bear sad tidings from the lower realms."

Hamilton, with a hundredweight of flour poised in midair, opened his mouth and gaped at me, and with all that dust flying about, I was afraid he might choke to death, so I decided not to waste my wit on him and got straight to the point. "Margaret won't be available all week," I told him, "because she is going to commune with nature and the dickybirds and not talk to a soul, so that she will become inspired and write a great work."

Hamilton slowly lowered the sack of flour, ruminating like a soulful Jersey cow, while he digested this bit of information. "What's she want to go and do that for?" he asked at last, petulantly.

"Because," said Julian, "she hopes to be a writer, and everyone knows that writers are a little bit nuts in the head, so you'd better respect her genius, or she'll think you're a Philistine." He indicated me with a jerk of his thumb. "That's her word, so if you want to know what it means, ask her."

Luckily he didn't, being rather slow on the uptake. "So you do understand, Hamilton, don't you?" I said sweetly. "If you want to take a genius out, you must be prepared to accept her funny little ways, right?"

"I suppose so," agreed Hamilton, and having suddenly discovered the use of the English language, added slyly, "How about you, then?"

Now it was my turn to goggle. "Oh, no!" I said hastily, fending him off with one hand while I made desperate gestures behind my back with the other for Maxwell and Julian to help me out. "You see I'm a bit weird, too."

"You bet she is," said Julian, rising to the occasion. "You know how on rainy days all the worms crawl out onto the roads. Well, she can't bear to think of them getting run over, so she picks them all up and puts them in her pockets until the sun comes out again."

"And she's always trying to lose weight," confided Maxwell, really in his element now, "so she eats all her meals standing on her head, because she figures the food will go the other way then, and she'll get a fat head, but that won't matter because her hair will hide it."

There were no half measures with my brothers. They either helped you with a vengeance, or they didn't help you at all. We had been slowly backing out of the mill all this time, while Hamilton looked on speechless, and once we reached the door, we fled for our cycles and got away from there as fast as we could.

"Imagine our Hamilton a wolf!" I chortled. "Don't you dare tell Margaret that he propositioned me, or we'll never get our twenty-five dollars."

"We'll never get it anyway, if your stupid plan doesn't work," growled Julian. But it did, only too well. Hamilton didn't come back at all, and in the end Margaret had to go and get him, and waste a whole evening trying to persuade him that insanity didn't run in the family. But we earned our money, and with my share of it I bought shorts, sneakers, and a bikini on sale, so that in spite of everything John didn't have to be ashamed of me.

Then, too quickly, the summer was over and John was gone, back to his vet school in Guelph. Now I had no riding to take my mind off him, and I was very lonely. I, who had goofed off for a whole year, suddenly found relief in schoolwork. Thanks to Mrs. Williams, I had made up my

English test, and now I flung myself desperately into all my lessons, finding that the harder the problem, the more occupied my mind became, and the less likely to wander into thoughts of what might have been. My back was improving slowly, but I wasn't allowed to do physical training or sports of any sort, and at school I was looked upon as a bit of an oddity, but I didn't care. We had always changed schools so often, before Father had settled down, that I was used to being an outsider. Father, at any rate, should have been pleased, but there were times when I caught him looking at me thoughtfully, and I couldn't help wondering if he missed the time when his youngest daughter had been acclaimed in riding circles as the young hopeful of the year and he had been able to bask in my reflected glory. We never talked about it, however, and I thought I had become resigned again to a dull monotonous life until the first cold winds of November swept the last leaves from the trees, and it was time once again for the annual Royal Horse Show and Winter Fair in Toronto.

This was to have been my special time, and now it really hurt. There were moments when I could hardly draw a breath for the longing inside me. I would have given years of my life to be able to go back to the day when my father had ordered me to give up my Saturday-morning job. How unimportant that loss of a few dollars seemed to me now, and how wise I was after the event. To make it worse, Mr. Holmes, who had a permanent box at the show, invited us all to be his guests on opening night. It was a full-dress, very élite affair, and tickets were very much in demand. My family, who could not be expected to pamper me forever, were all very excited. Even Maxwell and Julian decided it was worth getting scrubbed and polished for. Only I refused the invitation. To see it all happening before my eyes, and know that I was no longer part of that world was more than I could bear.

"I think you're crazy, Joanna," Mother said. "It's going to be a wonderful evening, and you'll get the feel of it, so you'll know what to expect when it's your turn."

Everyone was buzzing around getting ready, and I was in a very pessimistic mood. "It'll never be my turn now," I said with great pathos. "I had my chance and I blew it. Chances like that don't come twice. Mr. Holmes will get somebody else to ride for him next year, you'll see."

"Oh, Joanna, don't talk like that!" retorted Mother impatiently. She was trying to be in ten places at once, getting herself ready, supervising Julian and Maxwell, and placating Father. He had taken his tuxedo out of mothballs to air and Blob had sat on it, as he had a way of doing. Now it was covered with gray and white cat hairs, and Father was rampaging around, threatening to exterminate Blob and every cat that threatened to show a whisker within a mile's radius of our house. Eventually Grandma and Mr. Archer, who were also going, arrived, and with their help Mother managed to remove the pepper-and-salt look from Father's suit, and attend to any other minor crisis that erupted, such as when Margaret's earrings fell down the heat register, and Maxwell suddenly went on strike because Mother wanted to use hairspray on him.

So, with all this going on, nobody really had time to notice how staunchly and bravely I was bearing up, and I felt very much like Cinderella in my old jeans and sweater when finally everyone congregated in the kitchen before departing.

"Sure you won't change your mind, chicken?" asked my father. "You know you're going to be sorry afterward."

"Oh, it's too late now!" wailed Margaret. "If we have to wait for her to get changed, we'll never be on time."

"Don't worry," I said haughtily. "I won't spoil your evening. Just go and enjoy yourselves and forget about me."

The trouble was that they did, literally. Before they even drove away, they were laughing and joking, jostling each other for places in the two cars, ours and Grandma's, which Margaret was driving, and I had ceased to exist for them. It was no fun being a martyr with no one to notice me. I was alone in the empty house with only the animals for company. I didn't know what to do with myself. I read and did some knitting, and made myself a sandwich; I fed the dogs and tried to get interested in television and made myself another sandwich. I went down to the barn to talk to Horse, and found her leaning against her stall door, asleep with Horse the Second sprawled at her feet. She took the carrot I gave her without opening her eyes, and went on sleeping. I went back into the kitchen, made myself another sandwich, and wondered how long it would take to die of boredom, and whether it would be preferable and less painful than dying of a broken heart.

In the end I felt trapped and hemmed in. I couldn't stand it a moment longer, or I would scream. I put the dogs in the sun porch, seized my jacket, and fled the house, almost as though some dreadful fiend were after me. The weather didn't help my state of mind. A damp November fog settled in hollows in the road, and bare trees dripped dismally after a brief rain shower. An owl called far off somewhere behind the barns of Holmwood Farms, and it seemed to personify all the lonesome longing of all the lonely people in the world. A car swept by, quite indifferent to me, its headlights great monster orbs gobbling up the darkness, and when it had gone, the blackness was blacker still, the loneliness even more lonely. Two miles began to seem like an awfully long way. After my long period of enforced idleness, I wasn't in very good shape. I had done nothing more strenuous than cycle into the village for four months, and when I finally reached the little stone cottage snuggled by the side of the road, I was puffing like a steam engine. The red curtains shed a warm welcoming glow out into the night, and I was so anxious to be inside among the company of people again that I banged so heavily on the door I must have scared Mrs. Williams out of her wits. She came running to the door, and judging by the look on her face, she must have been expecting an accident or something terrible to have happened. Instead there was only me.

She took one look and said fervently, "Oh dear, no! Don't tell me you've run away again, Joanna!"

I was so pleased to see her, I found myself babbling incoherently, "Oh, no, I haven't, but my family's all gone to the Royal, and I'm alone and I'm going nuts! Please, can I come in and stay for a while? I'll even talk about horses if you want to, but don't send me home! I can't stand to be alone tonight—not tonight!"

Mrs. Williams was certainly a very placid person. You would have thought she had hysterical teen-agers on her doorstep every night. She didn't turn a hair. Instead she opened the door wide, gave me a big smile, and said, "Come on in, Joanna. The girls and I are making hot cider and cinnamon toast, and you're just in time to join us."

Birth of an Idea

INSIDE the cottage with the night shut out, it was even cozier than in the daytime. There was a little old Franklin stove in the corner of the kitchen, the kind where the doors open out to show the flames, and Kathy and Dinah were sitting beside it in their nightgowns making toast. On the top, a fragrant pot of cider garnished with orange and lemon rings and sticks of cinnamon simmered away, filling the kitchen with a delicious smell. They welcomed me like a long-lost member of the family. In no time at all, I was feeling human again, insulated by this bright little room and the laughter of the children from all the gloom and melancholy outside. Soon I was chattering away as merrily as any of them, and I wasn't even offended when Dinah said, "I think you're crazy not to have gone to opening night at the Royal, Joanna. It's fantastically hard to get in, even if you have tons of money. I'd love to see it. The Mounties do the Musical Ride, and all the women are dressed up in diamonds and furs and things. It must be super. I'd give anything to be there right now."

Personally I was quite happy to be where I was, but she couldn't be expected to know how I felt, so I only smiled and said nothing.

"Did your mother wear diamonds and furs?" asked Kathy innocently.

I thought of my mother frantically trying to let out her ten-year-old evening dress with stripes of a contrasting color, and sifting through Margaret's junk jewelry to find something that might conceivably look like gold and turquoise if you didn't look too closely, and I said, "No, not really. She's more the simple, elegant type."

Dinah sighed dreamily. "It sounds super. Mr. Holmes must be awfully disappointed that you won't be entering this year. How come he doesn't ride himself? He can't be that old, can he?"

I was surprised that she didn't know, but then I hadn't known once, either, until Grandma had told me. "He has an artificial leg," I said. "He was wounded very badly during the war. Before that, he had been one of the top riders in the country. That's why he always wanted John to be the best because, in a way, he was living his life through John. If John didn't come up to expectations, Mr. Holmes used to take it personally as though he himself had failed, and that's what made it so hard for John. He couldn't take it in the end, and that's why he left."

My story had subdued them all. "Poor man," said Mrs. Williams at last. She poked at the fire and said thoughtfully, "Somehow, whenever I drive past a place like Holmwood Farms, I can't help envying the people who live there because they're so much more fortunate than we ordinary mortals, but sometimes they're not, after all."

Grandma had once said exactly the same thing to me before I had got to know the Holmeses better and used to drool over how lucky they were. "Anyway," I said cheerfully, "it worked out for the best. Mr. Holmes changed completely after John left and became much nicer. Now he and John are the best of friends. My grandmother lived next door to him for years before she married again, and she says she's never seen him so content."

"Well, that's good," said Mrs. Williams, "but maybe Joanna doesn't feel like talking about it any more, Dinah. She can't be feeling too happy about it herself, you know."

Funnily enough, though, I was feeling better than I had for months. It was actually doing me good to talk about it. In fact I couldn't stop. I told them that naturally Mr. Holmes was disappointed about me, because he had had great hopes for Queenie, but he had other entries—two three-year-olds particularly who were to be shown on the line, not under saddle—whom he had great hopes for. They were judged for conformation and quality, and might add the Governor General's cup to the impressive collection of trophies in the library at Holmwood House.

"So I wasn't his only hope," I said with a wistful smile, "but I hope he wins something, I really do, because he's a terrific person and he hasn't had a very easy life."

It was only then that I realized for the first time in months, I was actually thinking of someone besides myself, and in comparison with the tragedy that Mr. Holmes had suffered, my own misfortune seemed like nothing. How would it feel to know that you would never ride again, never feel the butterflies in your stomach at the first sight of a difficult course, the supreme thrill of triumph when it was over and you had done well? The cheers from the crowd would never again be for him, and yet however much it must hurt to see others wearing the laurels that should have been his, he had not turned his back on horses. Instead he had built up one of the biggest breeding stables in the country.

It gave me food for thought. I had not even been able to bring myself to go and see Queenie after my accident. We had made such a lovely team, she and I. Now suddenly I wanted to see her again, fling my arms around her proud neck, and stroke her golden mane. I wanted to beg her forgiveness for ignoring her. I had a sudden, horrible feeling that she might have forgotten me.

My mood communicated itself to Dinah and Kathy, and they were much quieter as they contemplated the dying fire in the stove. Mrs. Williams said she thought it was time they went to bed.

"Oh, can Joanna stay the night?" begged Kathy. "Dinah and I can share a bed."

Mrs. Williams shook her head, laughing. "You seem to have yourself a fan club, Joanna, but I think I'd better take you home, don't you?"

I would have liked to have stayed, but I hadn't left a note for my parents, and since they wouldn't be back until after midnight, I could hardly expect Mrs. Williams to stay up and keep phoning until she got them. Still I hated to keep bumming rides from her. This would be the third time I had landed on her unexpectedly and she had chauffeured me home. "I can walk," I said, trying to shut out of my mind that stretch of lonely, desolate road. "I don't mind, really!"

She wouldn't hear of it. She shooed Dinah and Kathy off to bed and said with a bright smile at me, "We'll have a cup of cocoa and a bit of grown-up talk, shall we, and then I'll run you home? We haven't been here long enough to make many friends yet. Kathy and Dinah are good company for me, but sometimes I get a bit lonely for some adult conversation in the evenings."

She couldn't have said anything more calculated to raise my morale. At home I was always bracketed with Julian and Maxwell as the juvenile member of the family, while Margaret lorded it over us all by virtue of being the first-born, which was only a matter of lucky timing, that's all. Now that we were alone, and she wasn't giving me lessons, so we didn't have the pupil-teacher relationship to hamper us, I found myself getting along famously with Mrs. Williams. We talked about all sorts of things, including Dinah and Kathy. She was afraid the recent drastic changes in their life might have an upsetting effect on them.

"Dinah tells me she's in the same grade as your brother, Julian," she said. "Do you know if they seem to be settling down all right at school?"

"Oh I'm sure they are," I said reassuringly. "Julian says Dinah's doing just fine." What he had actually said was "Yuck, another girl in the class!" but I thought that in this case the truth was not called for, and she seemed relieved.

"I'm glad, although it's Kathy who worries me more than Dinah. She's a sensitive child, and she can't seem to understand that because her father and I are divorced, he still cares for her. It might help if they could see each other more often, but he's living in Vancouver now, and it's not possible. I'd like to see her get involved in something to get her mind off it, something she could really get excited about. I wish there was a riding school near here. I know when I was a girl, if anything worried or depressed me I always had my pony."

Her eyes took on that faraway, dreamy look that I had noticed when she first saw Othello. "His name was Buster Bill, and he was the cutest little fellow. I don't know what I would have done without him. He made growing up so much easier for me. In England the girls had their own ponies, but of course that's all changed now. I'd like to get them a horse one day, because we have ten acres here, but that's out of the question financially at the moment."

It made me sad to hear her talk like that, and now I realized what she had meant when she said I was lucky. And maybe I was lucky after all. Things were beginning to take on a different perspective for me. I wanted very much to cheer her up.

"I wouldn't worry too much about them," I said, trying to sound hearty and reassuring. "I had to move around all over the place before Father decided to settle down, and it didn't do me any harm." Then, remembering my behavior over the last few months, I wondered if I was such a good example to quote after all, so I added hastily, "At least I could have been a lot worse."

I had made her laugh anyway. She leaned across the table and gave my hand an affectionate squeeze. "You're all right, Joanna. You're good for us, you know that? I know you've been through a bad time, but I'm glad to see you're getting over it."

I lowered my eyes, feeling myself blushing. "I guess you understand why I took Othello, don't you?" I said awkwardly. "It seems silly now, but at the time, I had to—I just had to! I had to get away. I had to ride fast, and he was so big and strong it seemed as if he could push everything away, until there was only me and him left."

Mrs. Williams nodded her head, smiling. "Othello, the gentle giant," she said softly. "I thought he was lovely, too. I wonder if they've sold him yet."

I was ashamed to have to tell her again that I didn't know. I hadn't a clue what was happening at Holmwood Farms; and suddenly that, too, seemed shameful. I thought I had learned to live with the blow that fate had dealt me, but in reality I hadn't accepted it at all. All I had done was to build a protective wall about myself, shutting everything out that might hurt. Now that wall was breaking down, and I knew I had to go to the stables again and see Queenie and Othello, too, no matter how hard it was for me to do so. I was fed up with hiding. I wanted to be part of the real world again, the world that had been once so full of fun and promise.

I don't know if Mrs. Williams guessed how I was feeling, but she didn't raise any questions when I suddenly feigned tiredness and asked if she would mind taking me home.

The house was still in darkness, and the dogs set up a chorus of outraged barking because for a few hours they had been obliged to sleep on the floor like normal dogs, instead of on our beds.

"Will you be all right, dear?" Mrs. Williams asked me as I got out of the car. "I'd stay with you, but I don't like to leave the girls alone for too long."

"I'll be fine," I said. "You don't have to worry about me. And thanks for everything."

I meant that more than she knew. I watched the red taillights of her car disappear around a bend but instead of going into the house, I ran across the backyard and climbed over the fence. The furious squeals and yaps of the dogs faded into the distance, but for once they would have to wait. Although I hadn't been to Holmwood Farms for five months, it had once been such a part of my life, my feet had worn their own path through the fields, and I could have found my way blindfold. The barn was quiet, as I let myself in, with the comfortable, shuffling, snuffling noises of animals sleeping in the darkness all around me. I sniffed the warm barn smells and felt like the prodigal son returning home. I turned on the light nearest the door and heads reared up, dark liquid eyes looking at me curiously over wooden partitions. It was so good to be back again, I felt like singing out loud.

Queenie's stall was near the far end. I let myself in, and she turned and stared at me; then she waggled her bottom lip and stretched her neck, and it was just as if she were saying "Hey, about time, too! What happened to you?"

Laughing, I threw my arms round her and laid my head against her golden flank. "Oh, Queenie," I whispered. "I've missed you so much!" After that, we talked to each other for a long time, but what we said was a secret, understood only by Queenie and me. When I finally said good night to her, I felt full of hope and ready to start living again. To make it even better, as I passed the last box stall before switching off the light I saw a big, square muzzle pressed tightly against the bars and two black eyes rolling mischievously at me under a shaggy black forelock. So Othello hadn't been sold yet. Maybe Mr. Holmes was even going to keep him. The pieces of my life were falling back into place again, and maybe all the unhappiness I had been through hadn't been without a purpose after all.

Walking back across the fields, the idea came to me suddenly in a blaze of inspiration. I was so enthralled by it, the fog and the damp drizzle ceased to exist. I was totally oblivious to anything else. Back at the house I let the dogs out and Blob in, then Blob out and the dogs in, but hardly knew what I was doing. I was too tired to wait up for my family, so I went to bed, but even then I lay awake, too excited to sleep. I must have dozed off at last because I didn't hear my family come home, and when I woke up a cold November sun was streaming into my room, a family of migrating ducks was complaining loudly on our pond, and Blob was hurtling himself against the house and scratching the screen door to ribbons because nobody would get up and let him in.

Cautiously, tentatively, I felt my way around the idea again. It still seemed good. In fact it seemed more than good. It was the best idea I had ever had in my life. I felt bubbly inside, alive again for the first time in five months. The dogs were whining hopefully around my feet as I dressed, and this time I let them come with me. Everyone else was still asleep.

"Come on, dogs!" I sang out. "We've got important things to do. We've got to see Jim."

We were a happy procession as we ran across the fields. The dogs were puppyish, even great Jumbo chasing his tail in a ridiculous fashion. They must have caught my enthusiasm, and even my back seemed to be getting better because I didn't feel a single twinge all the way over to Holmwood Farms.

The Riding School

JIM HAD been to the Royal the night before, but he was up the same as usual, whistling between his teeth as he cleaned out the stalls in the big barn. There was nothing tired about the way he greeted me as I came running along the aisle followed by the three dogs. He leaned on a stall door, pushed back his cap, and surveyed me with twinkling eyes. "Well, now, who can this stranger be? The face looks familiar."

I had no time for games. "Jim," I cried, "I've got a great idea! A really marvelous idea!"

"I've got a good idea, too, sweetheart. Why not stop pretending you're an invalid and get back to work, so's I don't have to do your job on top of mine on Saturday mornings?"

"Jim, I'm serious. I want to start a riding school."

That knocked the teasing out of him. He closed the

door of the stall behind him, bolted it with agonizing slowness, then leaned on it, arms crossed, and said, "You what?"

"I want to start a riding school, Jim. I was talking to Mrs. Williams yesterday—that's the woman who was coaching me in English—and she wants her daughters to learn to ride, but there isn't any school near here. There must be lots of people like her, and here you have a covered arena and everything. It's perfect for a riding school! And think of the extra money you'd make. You know Mr. Holmes had to cut down on his stable last year because of the cost of feed and everything going up—well, this could be an extra income for him. It's a terrific idea, Jim! I could teach the beginners, and you could teach the more advanced riders, and we could really make something big out of it. Half the time the arena isn't being used anyway, and it's such a waste. I don't see how we could lose!"

Jim continued to look at me in that infuriating, passive way he had, when I was longing to communicate my excitement to him. "I'm really serious!" I exclaimed again. "This isn't a wild, hare-brained idea. This could be a moneymaker for Mr. Holmes!"

At last he allowed himself a smile. "So you've promoted yourself to be Mr. Holmes's financial advisor now, have you? Does he know?"

"Oh, Jim!" I was getting irritable. "You know I have to talk to you first because if you didn't go for it, he wouldn't. He always takes your advice. Couldn't we just talk about it?" I begged, feeling my hopes collapsing, feeling there must be something wrong with me because my ideas always seemed so marvelous to me, but never to anyone else.

Jim was very patient. He had a morning's work ahead of him, and he must be thinking I was a pain in the neck, but he put his hand on my shoulder and said with barely the trace of a sigh, "Okay, Joanna. Come into my office, and we'll talk about it."

Feeling more than a bit deflated, I followed him through the barn to the cubbyhole at the end beside the tack room, where Jim attended to all the paperwork involved in running a large breeding stable like Holmwood Farms. The whitewashed walls were covered with photographs of past winners of ribbons and trophies, pictures of horses jumping and of meetings of the Hunt Club, going back years before I was born. There was even a picture of Mr. Holmes, looking very young and happy and extraordinarily like John, when he had won the International Jumping Stakes in 1939. Among all those greats, I felt very audacious for being there at all, trying to tell Jim how to run his business.

He cleared a chair for me and sat down behind the cluttered desk. "Now, sweetheart, what's this you have in mind about a riding school?"

I told him, less ebulliently this time, what a good idea I thought it was, because as far as I knew, there wasn't another riding school any nearer than Kitchener, which was miles away, and there must be lots of parents like Mrs. Williams who would like their children to learn how to ride, or even take it up again themselves.

Jim considered this, rolling a chewed-up pencil between thumb and forefinger. "And which horses did you have in mind for a riding school?" he asked at last. "You can't use good horses on beginners. You'd ruin them in no time flat. Put twenty or so beginners on a horse like Queenie, for instance, even if they could handle her, and she'd soon be so full of bad habits you'd never be able to show her again. Her value would drop to nothing. No one serious about showing would buy her, and that's how we make our money——by breeding and selling. We're talking in thousands of dollars, Joanna. And if you have to start buying school horses, they have to be fed and cared for and vetted, all additional expense when we're trying to cut down on the number of horses in the stable. I'm sorry, Joanna, I don't think it feasible."

I refused to be cut down so easily. "All right," I countered. "Suppose you didn't have to buy any horses, and didn't use your show horses, either. What about Spirit, for instance? She's getting on now, and she's a broodmare, so you're not going to show her. You taught me to ride on her, and she was nice and gentle. And there's Cleo and Desert Lady and Zelda, all broodmares, and if you're cutting down on the number of horses, you won't be breeding so much, will you? So they might just as well be put to some use. And for the very beginners," I added in a moment of inspiration, "you could even use Horse. I mean nobody could ever be scared on her." I was firing myself up again with enthusiasm, remembering Kelp, John's first pony, kept in the stable for sentimental reasons, sixteen years old now but still full of pep. He would be great for the smaller children, like Kathy. "And then there's Othello!" I said, leaning forward in my eagerness to convince Jim. "I know he doesn't belong to Mr. Holmes, but he might as well earn his keep while he's waiting to be sold. I wouldn't trust him outside without an experienced rider, but in the arena he'd be marvelous. He does anything you ask him. He's fantastic."

Jim was smiling, anyway, a step in the right direction. "Hey, steady on, there! You're making my head spin. Othello does belong to Mr. Holmes now, by the way. The fellow who owned him needed the money, so Mr. Holmes bought him. But not to keep," he added, seeing my eyes light up. "We paid twelve hundred dollars for that ornery horse that cost me a year's work when he threw you, and Mr. Holmes wants his money back and then some. He'll make a good horse for someone who can handle him. Fifteen hundred we're asking for him. Meanwhile he's costing us a fortune every day, the amount he eats."

"There you are then!" I cried, clapping my hands together gleefully. "Let him earn his keep while he's staying here! And if you use Horse, Grandma and Mr. Archer wouldn't want you to buy her, I know. They'd be glad to have her over here, because they're both getting on a bit now, and that way they could see her whenever they wanted, without the trouble of looking after her. She has to be separated from Horse the Second soon, now he's getting to be such a big boy, so she might just as well come over here. And she'd earn her keep all right, and get her weight down, too. She'd be everybody's pet." I was running out of steam, and I felt quite exhausted. "Oh, please, Jim!"

I begged. "Couldn't you just consider it, enough to talk it over with Mr. Holmes anyway?"

I thought he was never going to answer. At last he stood up, came around the desk, and looked down at me, his weatherbeaten face deeply etched in thoughtful lines. "This means a lot to you, doesn't it, sweetheart?"

"Yes, Jim," I said. "I was trying to put horses right out of my life, but I can't."

"Well, I knew that," he said smiling. "Anyway I think you'll be riding again before too long, but it's good to see you taking an interest in things again. I'll tell you what I'll do. Mr. Holmes is staying in Toronto for the duration of the Royal, and I've got to go back Tuesday for our two entries, so I'll put the idea to him then, feel him out so to speak, and next weekend you can talk to him yourself."

"Oh Jim—!" I was so grateful I could think of nothing else to say.

"Now beat it!" he said, waving me away. "You've messed up my morning good and proper with your crazy ideas. And take those mutts of yours with you!"

"Yes, sir!" I cried happily as I scrambled for the door, calling to the dogs. "And don't pretend you're such an old grouch!" I flung back at him mischievously. "Because to me you're number one person!"

He liked that, even though he pretended to lose patience with me.

I took off back for the house, and then began the longest week of my life. I had really set my heart on having the school, now. It would be a wonderful way to earn money, even though I wouldn't expect much at the beginning, and it would be fun, too, meeting new people and making new friends, all with the same interest in riding. I was dying to tell someone about it, but I had a superstitious fear that if I did, it would all come to nothing; so I held my tongue and nearly burst inside, keeping it to myself during those seven endless days.

My family were still treating me with kid gloves. They played down their night at the Royal for my benefit, but I knew they had been impressed. I overheard Margaret discussing it with Hamilton.

"There must have been enough jewels there to buy the Taj Mahal," she told him dreamily. "Oh, Hamilton, wouldn't it be wonderful to be rich, and never have to worry about money ever again in your life?"

"Yup," answered Hamilton with about as much enthusiasm as a hibernating turtle. After his brief encounter with me at the mill, the art of conversation seemed to have deserted him again.

Saturday afternoon came at last, and I had to go back to the doctor for some more X rays. When I came home, Maxwell and Julian were waiting for me with the news that Mr. Holmes had phoned and would like to see me.

"What have you done now?" asked Julian.

"Why must I always have *done* something?" I cried in exasperation. "Isn't it possible that just once someone might want to see me for the pleasure of my company?"

"No," said Maxwell, looking up from the model ship he was building. "It's not possible."

"No one asked you," I said. "And you've got those sails on backward."

"No, I haven't," said Maxwell. "The sails are all right. It's the boat that's backward."

It was no use trying to treat them like human beings. I marched out huffily, and went across to Holmwood House to get it over. I knew that the two three-year-olds which Mr. Holmes had entered in the show had both won awards, so I hoped he would be feeling in a generous mood toward the world, and toward me in particular. All the same my knees were quaking as I rang the doorbell and was let in by Mrs. Bentley, the housekeeper. She showed me into the big blue-and-gold octagonal room where the French windows caught the last rays of the sun.

Mr. Holmes stood up to greet me. "Well, Joanna, this is like old times. I'll get Mrs. Bentley to bring us some tea."

I sat down beside the roaring fire in one of the sumptuous velvet chairs and congratulated him shyly on his success at the show.

"Yes, we did very well," he agreed, smiling at me. "But not as well as we'd hoped, of course. How's your back coming along?"

I told him I'd been to the doctor, who seemed to be pleased with my progress. Mrs. Bentley brought tea in on a silver tray, and we ate little cakes and made small talk, while all the time I was seething with impatience inside, wanting to get up and scream, "Tell me what you've decided!" Only, of course, I couldn't. You did things like that at our house, not in the elegant living room of Holmwood House. I had almost despaired of his mentioning it, and wondered if Jim had thought better about telling him or, worse still, had thought it so unimportant that he had forgotten to mention it. Then, quite casually, Mr. Holmes said, "So you want to start a riding school here, do you, Joanna? Well, that's not a bad idea."

I was so taken aback, so prepared to have to argue endlessly for my case, that I just stared at him with my mouth full of cake and squeaked, "It's not?"

He laughed. "You don't sound convinced. To tell the truth, I've toyed with the idea myself once or twice, since I started teaching you. I've derived a great deal of pleasure from our lessons together, but I think I've told you that before, haven't I?"

I was humbled and speechless. I felt such a boor for having stayed away so long. Mr. Holmes had been so good to me, and he must have thought I liked him only because of the riding, when it wasn't like that at all. And here I was again, asking another favor. I felt I had to try and explain that I hadn't avoided him for any personal reasons, only because I had been so mixed up and unhappy, but I got all tongue-tied in the process, and in the end he had to help me out.

"Don't worry about it, Joanna. When I was wounded during the war, I didn't want to see anybody, not even those nearest and dearest to me. When I knew I couldn't ride again, there was a time when I wished I could have been killed outright, but I got over it and knew you would, too. It's just a matter of time, that's all."

"But it was so much worse for you than for me," I said miserably. "I didn't have any right to treat everyone so badly when they'd all been so good to me."

"Well, that's all water under the bridge now, isn't it?"

Mr. Holmes gave me a friendly smile. "Between us, we've had to do a bit of soul-searching during the past year, Joanna, so let's just say we're quits and leave it at that. Now about this riding school, tell me what you had in mind."

I had been over it so often, I had everything planned to the last detail. First we should advertise in the local paper to see what response we got. Then, with one pony and five riding horses at our disposal, we could have several group lessons a week, an hour at a time, and half-hour private lessons if anyone wanted individual tuition. Children's lessons would have to be after school or on Saturdays, but adult lessons could be given by Jim in the evening, or in the case of housewives who didn't work, on weekday mornings after the barn chores were done.

Mr. Holmes considered my proposals gravely, nodding now and then to emphasize a point. I was so relieved to be taken seriously, I really excelled myself in the promotion of my idea.

"And you think there's a big enough need around here for a riding stable, do you?" he asked me as politely as if I were some big-shot business executive, instead of a nervous teen-ager with the shakes.

"Oh, I do!" I almost upset the silver tea tray in my eagerness. "I mean there's Kathy and Dinah Williams for a start, and there must be plenty more like them, even children with their own ponies who want to learn to ride properly so they can enter shows. And then there're the parents who used to ride like Mrs. Williams, who'd love to take it up again just for fun. I don't suppose it would make you a fortune, but I don't see how you could lose money on it."

Mr. Holmes regarded me with amusement. "Oh, I'm not too worried about making a fortune, Joanna. The government would only take it anyway. So long as the riding school pays its way, that's all I care about. Jim doesn't seem averse to the idea. He has more time on his hands now we've cut down on our breeding schedule. He'd probably enjoy it, but there might be a problem with your father if you start neglecting your lessons again. Do I have your word that won't happen?"

I nearly fell over myself, swearing black and blue, over my dead body, that I would be a paragon of virtue when it came to schoolwork in future. The amount of time I would spend giving lessons would be nothing compared to the hours I had spent riding before my accident. I could hardly believe it was settled as easily as that, but it was.

Mr. Holmes said to me, "It'll be a nice change to have something going on around here when I come home on the weekends. Since my father seems to like the sunshine in Florida and will probably stay down there, and John doesn't make it home too often, I sometimes wonder what I'm doing rattling around in this big house all alone." He bestowed his rather shy smile on me. "I've missed you over here, Joanna. I'd like to say welcome back."

"It's nice to be back," I said, and I meant it with all my heart.

There were a few more things to discuss, like how much he would pay me. We decided on five dollars for every lesson I gave, which seemed like a fortune to me. Even with a minimum of three lessons a week, that would still be fifteen dollars. My mind boggled at the idea of so much money at my disposal. Maybe, at last, I could open a bank account, something I had wanted to do for years, so that when financial emergencies arose, I would be ready for them. Regarding the ad in the paper, Mr. Holmes said he could never hope to compete with the fertile minds of my family, so he would leave it in our competent hands and all we had to do was send him the bill.

I was a bit heady with success when I left Holmwood Farms. A nip of frost was in the air, and the wind whistled up a few snowflakes that vanished like shooting stars in the corn stubble, but I felt so warm inside I wanted to open my arms wide and embrace the whole world. I stopped at our own little barn, built with our own hands, to say to Horse, "You are about to enroll in a riding school and become a school horse, so I hope you'll be on your best behavior and not make us ashamed of you."

Horse looked at Horse the Second and curled her lip, and I'll swear she was thinking, "Oh, boy, what next?"

"You big lazy lump," I told her. "It'll do you the world of good. You'll get your figure back and all the boys will fall for you."

I gave her a big hug around her neck and a sugar lump to console her; then I went into the house to break the news to my family that I was now in business.

I Have a Talk with Mrs. Williams

FOR ONCE my father actually seemed to approve of something I had done but whether it was because of my initiative or the fact that I would be financing myself in future, and he wouldn't have to have a guilty conscience about my allowance, I don't know. Anyway it was a good start, and my mother and Margaret were all for it, too. "It'll be nice not having you drooping around all the time for a change," Margaret said. "But don't try getting me to take riding lessons, that's all, because I'm just not a horsey person, and I never will be."

I assured her that I would struggle along without her, but meanwhile I needed Julian and Maxwell to help me compose the ad for the local paper. I corralled them up in the sleeping porch and said, "Now put on your thinking caps and come up with something really good, because a lot depends on this."

"How much are you going to pay us?" asked Julian.

"Nothing," I said. "I don't have any money until the riding school gets off the ground, and it won't if I don't come up with a good ad."

They sat on their beds and glowered at me. "How about 'Riding Lessons for Sale'?" said Maxwell without enthusiasm.

I looked at him in disgust. "Is that the best you can come up with? What's happened to your brilliant, inventive minds? Golly, when we had that stall at Kitchener Market to get money to build Horse a barn, you didn't have any trouble thinking up ideas then!"

"That was for all of us," said Julian, shrugging. "This is just for you. If the riding school's a success, you're the one who gets rich, not us."

I stood up, hands on hips, and really let them have it. "Why, you miserable, rotten so-and-so's! I suppose you want a cut. Well it was my idea, and you had nothing to do with it. All the times I've helped you out! I'll write my own ad. Don't bother!"

"Ten percent?" suggested Julian as I flounced out of the door.

I didn't even deign to answer. They were getting too mercenary for words. After a great deal of thumb-sucking and nail-biting, I came up with something I thought was striking enough without being too outrageous, and would appeal to all ages:

Is Your Life Humdrum, Blah, Uninteresting?
Put Some Spice into Your Living
Treat Your Family to Riding Lessons at
HOLMWOOD FARMS!

Underneath in small print, I added the details giving our phone number, and felt quite pleased with myself. I had intended to take it into the newspaper myself on Monday, as it was quite close to our school, but then I remembered my class was going on a field trip to the museum at Brantford, where Alexander Graham Bell had done his first experiments on the telephone. The newspaper came out on Wednesday, and Tuesday would be too late to catch that week's edition. My father was going to be away, so I asked Mother if she could borrow Grandma's car and take it for me.

"What's wrong with the boys taking it when they go to school?" she said. "They wouldn't mind, would you, Julian?"

"Nope," said Julian, doing his Hamilton-Schumacher routine.

"I don't trust them," I said sourly.

Julian shrugged. "What's to trust? If we say we'll take it, we'll take it, and that's that."

Maybe they were having guilt feelings about the shabby way they had treated me. If so, that was all right with me, but I wasn't a hundred percent convinced. "Swear you'll take it right to the newspaper office before school, and not forget it or anything like that," I demanded.

Julian struck a pose and said, "I swear it on the white hairs of my ancient grandmother."

"You'd better not let her hear you say that, or she'll bop you," I said, but I felt better about it. If they swore they would do something, they did it; in their own devious way they were quite honorable. "Don't forget to charge it to Mr. Holmes, and if it isn't in the paper on Wednesday, I'll kill you."

I went off to Brantford and had a good day at the museum, and Julian and Maxwell were as good as their word. The ad was in the paper on Wednesday, all right, but when I saw it, I nearly died. I let out a screech that brought the whole household running to see what dire new tragedy had befallen me. Distraught, running hands through my hair, I thrust the paper at my mother.

"Look!" I wailed. "Look what they've done to it! I'll be the laughing-stock of the neighborhood!"

Mother read the ad out slowly as it appeared in our local rag:

Is Your Wife Humdrum, Blah, Uninteresting?
Put Some Spite into Your Living
Treat Your Family to Riding Lessons at
HOLMWOOD FARMS!

Trying hard to hide a smile, she said, "They seem to have made a couple of printing errors, dear."

Seizing the paper, I rolled it up and brandished it at Maxwell and Julian, who ran for safety behind the chesterfield. "Printing errors, my foot! They changed it purposely! Now no one's going to take it seriously! I'm ruined before I start—absolutely ruined!"

They protested in vain that they had had nothing to do with it; that the typesetter at the newspaper was ninety years old and half blind, that the presses didn't work properly and were always making mistakes. I didn't believe a word of it. I had them by the ears and was banging their heads together, until Mother and Margaret pulled me off and tried to calm me down.

"We'll make them rerun it properly next week, dear, but I think it's funny. It'll make people laugh. There's no harm done."

"I'm ruined!" I wailed tragically. "Ruined, ruined, ruined!"

But, funnily enough, Mother was right. The phone hardly stopped ringing in the next two days. Most of the people just wanted to know if it was a joke or not, but some I got talking to and they became interested in having lessons, and some were interested anyway and thought the ad was hilarious. The only person who objected was a woman's libber who said it was antifemale propaganda and I ought to be prosecuted, but since she didn't seem to be in the market for riding lessons, I didn't worry about her.

The upshot of it all was that whether Maxwell and Julian were guilty or not, we got a whole raft of people, both children and adults, wanting lessons, and the riding school was no longer a pipedream but a reality. I had meetings with Jim and Mr. Holmes, and we decided to open in the new year, which would give us time to work with the horses concerned and school them for their new job. This would mainly fall on Jim, though John helped when he came home for the Christmas vacation; and one wonderful day, far better than any Christmas present I could have had, I got the news from the doctor that my back was so much better, I could try riding again, but only for short periods and I was not to jump or do anything reckless that might cause me to fall off again for the time being.

So I had my first ride after six months on gentle, plodding Horse, who had been transferred to Holmwood Farms, and the whole family was there to cheer me on. Jim, John, and Mr. Holmes were there, too, to give me encouragement. My heart was in my mouth as I mounted Horse and walked her slowly round the arena; then suddenly everyone was clapping and cheering and giving me wolf whistles. I don't think I could have felt prouder if I had won a trophy at the Royal.

Afterward I said to John, "Isn't it funny how you have to be unhappy first, before you can really appreciate being happy with little things, like riding Horse."

John smiled at me and said, "But maybe the little things like riding Horse are really the big things that matter, Jo, and we're all topsy-turvy." He was always saying wise little things like that, no doubt hoping to make me into a better, happier person, but I couldn't have been happier that Christmas if I had tried; and the new year was better still because that's when I gave my very first riding lesson to Kathy and Dinah Williams and four other children.

I stood in the middle of the ring like a pro, and made them walk the horses in single file with feet out of the stirrups and then I had them pick up their stirrups and knot the reins and walk around with their hands on their heads —all this so they would use their knees to stay on the horse, which is the basic principle of riding. By the end of the lesson they were trotting and posting, and I felt I had really achieved something. Jim sat in on the lesson to give me support, but afterward he said I was a born teacher, and he wouldn't worry anymore about supervising me, which pleased me no end. For once in my life, I seemed to be doing everything right, which was a good feeling.

Only one thing puzzled me. Mrs. Williams hadn't enrolled at the school. I had been so certain she would have been the first to enroll in the adult classes that I was disappointed. Dinah and Kathy were really enjoying themselves. They loved the riding, but even better they seemed to enjoy the friends they made. I used to watch them after the lessons, congregating in the barn with the other girls, discussing riding and shows, their faces bright and rosy with the exertion of the lesson, and it seemed to me that Kathy, particularly, was blossoming out. It was nice to see her chattering away, sparkling and animated. She and her sister were not particularly good riders, but they had spunk. Whenever they fell off, they mounted right away without tears or sulks, and they were a good example to the other children. At school they had been retiring and shy, but here where everyone shared a love of horses, they made friends quickly and were popular. Mr. Holmes, who used to pop into the barn regularly on Saturday mornings, to see how I was handling things, took a great fancy to them. For some reason he called them Tweedledum and Tweedledee.

"Come on, Tweedledum, smile!" he would sing out to Dinah, as she fought a losing battle to make Horse canter; or "What's the matter, Tweedledee? Have you lost your steering wheel?" as Kelp ran out of a jump three times in a row.

"I like Mr. Holmes," Kathy told me confidentially one morning. "I always thought somebody that rich would be kind of frightening, but he's not at all."

"I used to be frightened of him, too," I confessed, "until I found out he's one of the kindest persons in the world." Dinah had joined us, so I took the opportunity to ask what had happened to their mother.

Dinah shrugged. "I don't know, Joanna. She keeps saying she might start riding again, but that's all. Kathy and I wondered if maybe she's been away from it so long, she's a bit scared. Why don't you talk to her?"

Mrs. Williams didn't seem to me like the kind of person who would be scared of anything much, but there had to be a reason, so I promised I would drop over later after I had been down to our barn to see how Horse the Second and Tangles were doing.

Tangles was the newest addition to our menagerie, a frisky little lamb that Father had purchased at a livestock sale to keep Horse the Second company, now his mom had moved out. At first Horse the Second, in true family tradition, had sniffed at her and tried to eat her, but finding her inedible, they had settled down to a suspicious friendship. Father had great plans for getting Mother a loom so that she could weave and knit all our winter sweaters from Tangles' wool, but, as Mother had said, "We'd better fatten her up a bit then, because right now I doubt if you'd get one sock off her."

When I went into the barn, Horse the Second was standing up in his stall with a long-suffering look on his face, while Tangles pushed and nosed at his tummy, trying to get a drink of milk. The tables seemed to have been reversed, and the fact that Horse the Second was enduring it and not kicking out at her with his sharp little hoofs seemed like a good omen.

I took hold of his muzzle, and blew gently down his nostrils. "Your mom sends her love," I told him, "and hopes you're being a good boy and enjoying your new friend." He pulled his head away and butted me out of his stall, which was as good an answer as any; but in spite of the indignities he had to suffer, he seemed to take a protective interest in Tangles, and our worries that he might be lonely without Horse seemed to have been solved.

After lunch, I got out my bicycle and rode down to the stone cottage. Mrs. Williams seemed genuinely pleased to see me. She told me that Kathy and Dinah had been asked out to tea by one of their new riding friends. "That school's made all the difference in the world to them," she said, glowing at me. "It was a perfectly splendid idea, Joanna, and I can't tell you how happy I am for you, too."

"Well, indirectly you were responsible," I told her. "It was really *you* who gave me the idea, but I thought you'd be one of the first to join. We have adult classes in the mornings on Monday and Wednesdays, but if you're working, we have one on Wednesday evenings, too. Jim says they have lots of fun. After they've ridden, they all go up to the house, and Mrs. Bentley makes them coffee and it's more like a social club than a riding school."

Mrs. Williams smiled at my eagerness, but there was something wistful in her eyes. "It's not that I wouldn't like to, Joanna. I've changed my library hours to the afternoons now, so I could come in the morning, but it's not that. I just wonder if I can afford that kind of luxury for myself. Kathy and Dinah really needed something like that, to get the feel of belonging again, but for myself—I don't know. We make do, but we're not exactly rolling in money, Joanna. I just don't feel justified in spending that extra money on myself, when there are so many other things we need."

The money angle hadn't occurred to me, though it should have, seeing that my own family was constantly scraping the bottom of the barrel. My own plans had been hampered so often for lack of funds that I could sympathize with her. It was a frustrating business. I asked her if I could come in, and over tea and cookies I said that maybe I could get Mr. Holmes to make an exception in her case and give her a discount, since three members of her family would be riding, but she wouldn't hear of it.

"It's very kind of you, Joanna, but I don't want any special treatment. That's too much like charity. That's one thing I decided when we moved to the country and bought this little cottage, I don't want any favors from anybody. I knew it wouldn't be easy, but we're doing well enough. We're certainly far from starving, and I have my part-time job to supplement my income, but we still have to watch what we spend. A year's riding lessons for me would buy a lot of clothes for Kathy and Dinah."

I looked at her in exasperation; it was my own mother all over again. She was always putting the family before herself, making do and being self-sacrificing. I couldn't get anywhere with Mother when I tried to tell her that she was a person in her own right, because she adored my father and would have gone around in rags to make him happy, but with Mrs. Williams it was different. I was determined to have a try.

"I don't think you should think like that," I said as tactfully as I could. "Dinah and Kathy are going to grow up and go away, and then you're not going to have anything. They've got their whole lives in front of them. If you want riding lessons now, why shouldn't you have them, even if it means Dinah and Kathy have to go without a new dress or something? If you wait till they're grown up, you'll be too old and your whole life will have passed you by." She was looking at me, rather surprised, and I wondered if I wasn't being overly dramatic. Still, I had plunged in now and might as well go all the way. "I bet Kathy and Dinah would be the first to agree with me," I said. "They both want you to have lessons. My mother's the same as you. She's always putting us first, and sometimes she looks like a regular frump because she won't spend any money on herself. I love my mother, but I'd respect her a lot more if she'd stand up for her own rights."

I had startled Mrs. Williams all right; she wasn't used to being talked to by sixteen-year-olds like that, but I was really sincere, and I think she knew it. She laughed and shook her head, looking a bit bewildered.

"My goodness, Joanna, you'd make a good saleswoman. You really feel strongly about it, don't you? I've never thought about it like that. Children really want to be proud of their parents, don't they?"

"Well, not that so much," I said, self-consciously now.

"It's just that they don't like feeling guilty because their parents are always giving up things for them. You don't enjoy things so much if you know someone's had to go without because of you."

She took a deep breath, and suddenly her eyes were sparkling again like the first time she had seen Othello. I felt that she had really wanted somebody to talk to her like that. "All right!" she said with sudden resolution. "You've convinced me, Joanna! The children like hamburger better than steak anyway. I wonder if I can still get into my jodhpurs? Do you think I can have Othello?"

"He's right there," I said, laughing, "waiting for you!"

She was a different person when I left her. She looked ten years younger, and excited like a child with a treat in store. I went home, flushed with success, and thought I would try the same routine on my mother. I found her baking bread because Father didn't like the store-bought stuff. She had on an old housedress, and her hair was drawn back in a bandanna and hanging down her back in curly wisps.

"Mother," I said, approaching her. "Why don't you put your foot down and make Daddy take you out to dinner tonight for a change. Let him go without something for once, and put you first. We'd all respect you better, if you did."

"Oh, don't talk nonsense, Joanna," she said impatiently, "and stop leaning all over the table. You're in my way."

Father came in just then, sniffed the bread, put his arm round my mother, pinched her bottom, and said, "And how is the bread coming along, my sexy one? Don't forget

I want the crust hot. There's nothing in the world to beat a hot crust straight out of the oven."

"Yes, dear," said Mother. "Coming straight up."

You couldn't win them all, I suppose. I gave up in disgust and left them to it.

Mrs. Williams and Othello

TRUE TO her word, Mrs. Williams began lessons the very next Monday, and her love affair with Othello started in earnest. Jim told me it was really funny to see her handle that big powerful horse. In true school-marm fashion, if he acted up, she would dismount, look him face to face and say with a no-nonsense attitude that meant business, "Now we're being a naughty boy, aren't we, and it's going to stop right now, isn't it? Do you understand, Othello?" If he tried to toss his head or pull away, she yanked on his reins and made him look her in the eye. He just couldn't win. She was the boss right from the start. She loved him dearly, but she wasn't going to stand any nonsense from him, and he sensed it. Without using a crop or anything, she got her own way merely by being firm. Jim said he had never seen anything like it. "It's mind over matter," he told me. "Othello's a great school horse, but he can be ornery as the dickens when he's a mind to with anyone else. With her he's as meek as a lamb. I'll swear he thinks she's going to keep him in after school to write out a hundred times 'I will be good' if he doesn't do what she wants him to."

I soon had a chance to see for myself. I had a cold, enough to keep me home from school, but not enough to keep me indoors, so I went over to the arena to watch the Monday-morning lesson. Mrs. Williams brought Othello into the ring last, after the other ladies were mounted. She was bonnie and rosy from her walk across to the barn in the cold February air, and her skin-tight jodhpurs showed off her good figure. Othello was feeling his oats, tossing his head and fidgeting when she tried to get him to stand still to mount him. After trying unsuccessfully once or twice, I saw a steely look come into her eyes. She marched around until she was standing level with his nose and just stood looking at him. "Othello," she said at last, "you aren't being very nice. I haven't seen you for a week, and you seem to have developed some bad habits. Now I won't stand for that, so are you going to be good or not?" In front of my eyes, Othello capitulated. He became a meek, gentle, lovable horse, who did everything right all through the lesson.

"How do you do it?" I asked her afterward, when she was brushing him down in his stall. "Do you hypnotize him?"

She laughed merrily. "Of course not, silly! I just love him, that's all. Don't I, sweetie?" she said to him, tickling his chin.

I wasn't convinced. "Everybody loves Horse," I reminded her. "And the more you love her, the more she takes advantage of you." I knew, because I was riding Horse regularly now, to try and get back into shape, and it was a continual battle of wits. To get Horse to do anything faster than a slow amble I had to give her the crop hard, and then she obeyed with such long-suffering patience and sighs and snorts that I felt like a brute. But at least there wasn't much chance of her taking off with me, or doing anything stupid, except perhaps lying down on top of me and squashing me flat.

Anyway, Mrs. Williams was happy, and so were her daughters. She told me that Kathy had written to her father about her riding, and now there was a regular correspondence going between them. There was no more talk about not being loved, and she seemed to have accepted things as they were at last. That made me feel good. So many people had helped me, it was nice to feel that I had helped somebody else for a change. But, of course, I might have known it wouldn't stay that way for long. It never did. Whenever I was on top of the world, something always happened to tumble me right off again. The bombshell came when Jim told me that one of his Wednesday evening riders was interested in buying Othello. He was the father of Polly Jones, one of the children who took lessons from me after school. Polly had her own pony, and her father had taken lessons with the idea of buying a horse to keep her company. He had taken a fancy to Othello, because he presented a challenge, and there was no shortage of money in the family.

I stared at Jim aghast when he broke the news to me. "But, Jim, we can't let Othello go! He's one of our best school horses. We're short enough of good horses as it is."

Jim looked rueful. "Well, sweetheart, that's the way it is. You've known from the start that he's up for sale. Mr. Holmes has put a lot of money into that horse and he's not going to turn down an offer if the price is right. It's a shame to use a good horse like Othello in a riding school. Better to go to an auction sale and pick up a school horse for two or three hundred dollars."

I screwed up my face in anguish. "But, Jim, what will Mrs. Williams do without him?"

Jim laughed. "We'll have to give her Horse instead. Maybe she'll get the same results there. A good rider has to learn to handle all kinds of horses. You know that, Joanna. You can't call yourself a good rider, if you can only handle one horse."

He was right about that, but with Mrs. Williams and Othello it was different. I don't think she cared about being a good rider. All she cared about was Othello. I cornered Polly after her lesson and asked if it was definite her father was going to buy Othello. She told me he hadn't quite made up his mind, and he was going to look around a bit first. They didn't intend to buy until the summer, and Othello might just as well remain at the school where her father could ride him on Wednesdays through the winter, but so far he hadn't seen a horse he liked better. I went home that night very depressed.

"I'm going to see Mr. Holmes this weekend and ask him not to sell Othello," I declared to my assembled family at suppertime. "I'm sure he won't if I ask him not to."

My father gave me his bristling look. "Joanna, you will do no such thing! How many times do I have to tell you not to take advantage of friendship? What right have you to interfere in Mr. Holmes's business?—and selling horses is his business. I won't have it, I tell you! There's a limit to the amount of favors you can ask under the guise of friendship. Mr. Holmes has been very generous in giving you the facilities for this riding school, so don't push your luck or you may find he's getting just a little bit tired of having his affairs run by a teen-ager."

I scowled at him. "He isn't doing it for nothing. He's making money from the school."

Father gave a derogatory snort. "Peanuts, peanuts! After taxes I doubt if it even pays for the feed for those horses. I'm warning you, Joanna, you're going to go too far one day, meddling in other people's business."

"Yes, you'd better watch it," taunted Julian. "He could get so sick of you, he'll find a new rider for Queenie. He's got the riding school now to pick from, so you've got competition."

If they were trying to scare me, they succeeded. I didn't dare say another word, but I felt very sorry for Mrs. Williams. Julian's warning had made me realize how awful I would feel if some stranger came along and usurped my place with Queenie. There was an affinity between certain people and certain horses, and unless you had experienced it, it was hard to understand. All I could do was to keep my fingers crossed and hope desperately that before the summer came Mr. Jones would find a horse that appealed to him more than Othello.

I didn't say anything to Mrs. Williams, but the word

spread around, as it was bound to do. I met her one day as she came to pick up Dinah and Kathy after their lesson.

"What's all this I hear about Othello being sold?" she asked me, coming straight out with it.

I couldn't meet her eye. I mumbled something about it not being certain and that anything could happen in four months, but she wasn't to be put off so easily.

"How much do they want for him?" she asked, and there was the same purposeful set to her mouth that she got when Othello was being difficult.

"Fifteen hundred dollars," I said, feeling the words stick in my throat.

"I'm going to buy him," she said.

"You're what!" The eyes nearly rolled out of my head. "I thought you said you didn't have any money!"

"I don't," she said, looking grim. "But I want Othello, and I intend to get him. I've seen Mr. Jones ride him, and he just doesn't have the feeling for him that I do. He's not right for Othello. I've got four months to do it in. It won't be easy, but I've made up my mind!"

I was flabbergasted. She walked off with her head in the air and determination in every step, and I knew she meant business, though I didn't see how she could possibly do it. She hadn't felt she could afford the price of riding lessons, so how could she hope to buy a fifteen-hundred-dollar horse along with the facilities for keeping him?

I was soon to find out. The next Saturday when my lesson was over, Kathy and Dinah asked if they could walk home with me to say hello to Horse the Second and Tangles.

"Why sure," I said. "But isn't your mother coming to pick you up?"

Dinah shook her head. "She's got herself a job as an Avon Lady, and she's got to go all over the countryside selling perfume and stuff, so we have to get our own lunch."

"She's going to buy Othello, you know," Kathy said, looking at me owlishly. "She really means it, so she needs all the extra money she can get. Does your mother need cosmetics or anything?"

I looked down at her sadly. "I've news for you, Kathy. My mother doesn't have any more money than yours. The only difference is, she doesn't want to buy a horse." She looked crestfallen, until I remembered that I was in the money now. I had opened a bank account and already had fifty dollars in it, but I still couldn't get used to the idea that I wasn't broke. "Tell her to bring the catalogue around to me," I said, tasting the great feeling of being flush for the first time in my life. "I'll buy Margaret something for her birthday present, and I could do with some nice smelly stuff for when John comes home next time."

That cheered them up, and after we had visited with Horse the Second and Tangles, I told them they had better come home to have lunch with me. In my family, you never had to ask permission to bring people home. You just watered down the soup a little bit more and hoped for the best. Julian, Maxwell, and Margaret were already at the table, scoffing away when we came in.

"You two know each other of course," I said to Julian and Dinah. "Being in the same class and all."

Dinah batted her eyelids demurely and said, "Oh, yes! Everybody knows Julian. He's the most popular boy in the school!"

Well, if her mother knew how to handle horses, Dinah certainly knew how to handle boys. Julian stopped scooping up soup as though he hadn't eaten for days and stared at Dinah with her prim old-fashioned little face as if he had never seen a girl before. Then he actually stood up and brought a chair to the table for her while Maxwell and I watched in utter disbelief. As an afterthought he brought one for Kathy, too, and put it down for her next to Maxwell, who gave her a ghastly smile and bent once more to his soup as though he needed all the nourishment he could get to cope with this emergency. The spectacle of Julian being gallant was too much for the rest of us. We tried to be natural, but all we could do was gawk at him, while he chatted away to Dinah about school, passing her the bread and anything she wanted. Afterward he suggested they go skating.

"There's all kinds of old skates in the basement," he said. "There's bound to be some your size."

"Oh, that would be nice," agreed Mother enthusiastically. "Maxwell and Kathy can go as well. You'll have a lovely time together."

Maxwell began protesting vehemently that he had other plans, but Mother kicked him under the table, nearly crippling him, if the agonized look on his face was anything to go by. We found Kathy and Dinah skates and saw them off; then Mother, Margaret, and I went back to the kitchen and laughed so hard we thought we would die.

That was the first of many meals that Kathy and Dinah were to have at our house because Mrs. Williams really meant it when she said she was going to buy Othello. It wasn't such a lucrative business selling cosmetics to farmers' wives, and she had to go farther and farther afield, which meant that with her job at the library she was hardly ever home. She left Kathy and Dinah meals to heat up, but Mother felt sorry for them and kept asking them over to our place. Julian didn't seem to mind at all, and Maxwell gradually came to accept Kathy as a necessary evil that could, with an effort, be tolerated and even liked at times, when she and Dinah made homemade fudge in our kitchen or helped him with his homework. He stopped writing JULIAN LIKES GIRLS on walls and in snowbanks, and things settled down to normal.

One Sunday Mrs. Williams came over herself to thank us for being so kind to her girls, and to bring her samples. Margaret and I had a field day. We squirted ourselves with perfume and made ourselves up to look like clowns, then started on Mother. Mrs. Williams said the cosmetic business wasn't paying as much as she had hoped, because the cost of driving her car was eating up her commission, but she was lucky. She had answered an ad for a cleaning lady at the doctor's house, and gotten the job.

"You mean as well as selling this stuff?" asked Mother, blinking her heavily mascaraed eyes. "Surely you won't have time, not with your library job as well."

"Well, it's just one morning a week," said Mrs. Williams cheerfully. "Good household help is hard to find these days, apparently, so they pay well. I'm hoping the doctor's wife will recommend me to some of her friends." She laughed at our astonished faces. "I may not have too many talents, but I can scrub floors."

Mother took a tissue from the box on the table and carefully scrubbed at her face until she was down to bare skin again. "But what about Dinah and Kathy?" she asked. "You're not going to have any time with them at all."

Mrs. Williams shrugged philosophically. "Well it's only till the summer. Dinah and Kathy aren't little children anymore. They're quite responsible. If I'm out late, my neighbor keeps an eye on them for me, and they can always ring her up if they have any problems. It won't hurt them to learn to be self-sufficient."

Mother wasn't at all convinced. "Are you sure?" she said. "I believe that children should have a home life. It's very important to them."

"Now, please Mrs. Longfellow—" Mrs. Williams stood up and began packing her samples away. "For once in my life, I'm putting myself first, because getting Othello is important to me. I don't mean that Kathy and Dinah aren't, but I have a life of my own to live, you know. So long as I don't neglect them, and see that they're fed and have clean clothes, I don't think I need to have a guilty conscience. I've given thirteen years of my life to them, now surely they can give me four months without everyone calling me a bad mother. When Othello is ours, we can all enjoy him, so please don't try and make me feel like a criminal because of it."

She was quite worked up, and Mother was taken aback. At least she dropped the subject, and I was glad, because

Mrs. Williams had sounded exactly like me talking, and I didn't realize how persuasive I had been. I placed a ten-dollar order with her, because I was feeling a bit guilty myself, and after she had gone, my mother said, "I wonder where she gets ideas like that from. I don't understand these modern mothers. I hope you children appreciate how lucky you are having me at your beck and call all the time. What would you do if I decided to go out and get a job?"

I mumbled something unintelligible and made a hasty exit. There were times in my complicated life when the least said the better, and this appeared to be one of them.

We All Go to Work

I WAS SO busy during the winter months, I hardly noticed the passing of February, until the sun's rays grew warmer and the cawing of crows echoed over the snowy fields. March was upon me before I realized it. Farmers hung their sap buckets in the sugarbushes; the willows turned yellow; and the March school break was just around the corner. I had a riding course planned for the whole of that week to get my pupils in shape for the summer shows. Margaret was excited about the school break, too, because Father was in Toronto working on a documentary and he had invited Margaret to join him so that she could get firsthand knowledge of what went on in a television studio. Wallace had agreed to come down specially and take her back with him. Hamilton presented a slight problem, but she got around it by describing Wallace as an old family friend, somehow managing to give

the impression that he was doddery and senile, a
Hamilton worked on Saturdays, there was little c
their meeting anyway.

With everyone furiously planning things for the school break, Maxwell and Julian felt left out, and went around declaring that they were underprivileged. At last Mother threatened to put them on a diet of bread and water so their complaints would be justified. After that they shut up, and contented themselves with a few discreet mumblings for Margaret's and my benefit.

Kathy and Dinah didn't have much to look forward to, either. They couldn't afford the course, and since Mrs. Williams had taken on three other cleaning jobs, they wouldn't have anyone to take them anywhere. I had cycled into the village one evening to get some ice cream for dessert, and Maxwell and Julian had accompanied me. Before I was in the money, they wouldn't have been seen dead with me, but now it was different. Any time I went near the store they were on my heels. I suppose I was a sucker, but I couldn't stand to see them hanging around looking servile and wistful, and I always ended up buying them bubble gum or popcorn. As we cycled back, I suggested we pop in and say hello to Dinah and Kathy to cheer them up a bit.

Dinah's face lit up when she opened the door to our knock. "Oh, I'm so glad you've come!" she cried, almost dragging us in. "I'm just fed up with everything, and so is Kathy. She's threatened to write to Daddy and tell him to come and take us away, and I'm having the worst job persuading her not to. I don't want to spoil everything for

Mommy, but it's getting worse. I don't think she'll get Othello anyway, not now. Her car broke down four days ago, and it's cost her four hundred dollars to have it fixed, so she's almost back where she started."

I had no idea things were so bad. I hadn't been in the cottage since I had gone over to persuade Mrs. Williams to ride. Now I was shocked at the difference. It had been such a cozy little place then; now it looked neglected and forlorn, with dirty dishes still in the sink and dust on all the furniture.

"I know it's a mess," apologized Dinah as she showed us in. "Kathy and I tried to keep it clean for a while, but then we got behind with our homework, and Mommy told us not to worry. She said she'll have a real big spring cleaning when she gets Othello, and a bit of dust won't hurt us."

"She's too busy cleaning everyone else's houses to do ours," said Kathy bitterly. She was heating a pot on the stove and turned round indignantly to face us. "You know what? I had to go home with one of the girls at school last Monday to borrow a book, and we went into the kitchen, and there was my mother scrubbing the floor. I nearly died. I pretended not to know her, and she laughed in front of my friend and said I was a snob." She banged the lid down on the pot. "I'm sick of it! I'm just sick of it! I don't want Othello all that much. I mean he's a nice horse, but he's too big for us to ride anyway."

I didn't know what to say. I began to pick up papers and stack them in a pile, and I asked Julian to get a broom and start sweeping the floor, while I found a clean tablecloth to try and perk the place up a bit. Maxwell even got a duster and flicked it about, shifting the dust from one side to the other. Meanwhile Kathy and Dinah just eyed us listlessly, and Dinah said, "It's awfully nice of you to help, but it's going to get just as bad again, so you might just as well not bother. Now Mommy has to make up that four hundred dollars as well, she'll probably get a job as a night watchman, and then she'll never be home at all."

"I'm going to write to my father," said Kathy defiantly. "I don't care what you say, Dinah."

"Now, wait, wait!" I said, holding up my hand. "Let's talk about it. Let's not do anything hastily." I had visions of Family Court coming in and taking Kathy and Dinah away from Mrs. Williams because she wasn't a fit mother. Something had to be done. I made them sit down, and we all sat around in gloomy silence while I did some thinking. It wasn't easy, and I tried to talk myself out of it, but I knew in the end I was going to have to do it. I remembered the time when we had been looking after Horse while Mr. Archer had been in the hospital. His nephew had threatened to sell her without his knowledge, and we were so furious we had been obliged to kidnap Horse. It had worked out in the end, but only because John had helped us, and Jim, and Grandma. Without their help we would never have had Horse now, or Horse the Second. Now I was in a position to help someone else who loved and wanted a horse, and I couldn't refuse without despising myself. I had a hundred and fifty dollars in my bank account now, fifty dollars to come for the course I was giving next week, and with my weekly fifteen dollars from then on till the end of May, I estimated I would have around four hundred dollars by that time. Whatever it had done to my English, my mental arithmetic had certainly improved since I had been in the horse business.

Sadly bidding good-bye to the wonderful idea of Joanna Longfellow with a bank account of her own, I said to Dinah, "If the price of Othello dropped to eleven hundred dollars, do you think that would help? I mean at least your mother wouldn't have to make up the four hundred dollars for the car then, would she?"

I explained that I would give my money to Jim on the quiet and have him tell Mrs. Williams that the price had gone down, because I knew that she would never agree to it otherwise. I knew I could trust Jim not to say anything. He might not always approve of me, but when it came to helping people you could always rely on him.

Dinah looked quite shocked. "Oh, Joanna!" she cried. "We couldn't! We couldn't take your money!" Then suddenly her face sort of folded up, and tears were streaming down her cheeks. "You're just so kind!" she sobbed. "You're so kind, and there's no reason you should help us—none at all!"

I comforted her as well as I could and found her a Kleenex in all the muddle to blow her nose on. "There is a reason to help you," I said staunchly, "because everybody helped me when I was in trouble, and now it's my turn. I can start my bank account all over again once your mother has Othello, and a few months won't make any difference. I never had any money before anyway, so what else is new?"

Julian was very distressed to see Dinah in tears, and he was resentful that all the gratitude seemed to be going to me, while he was ignored. He cleared his throat to draw attention to himself and said importantly, "I could help you, too, if you like. I could give up my hockey on Saturday mornings and ask Jim if I can have Joanna's old job cleaning out the barns. It's only four dollars a week, but it's something."

That was a real sacrifice for Julian, because he was hockey mad, and now it was Maxwell's turn to be peeved. With Dinah and Kathy looking adoringly at Julian and me and showering us with thanks, he was the odd one out. He scuffed the floor with the heel of his shoe and said gruffly, "Guess I could help, too, if there was something I could do."

Suddenly it was like old times when we had banded together to save Horse, only now we were a team fighting together to save Othello. Nothing stirred the Longfellow blood like a good honest challenge. Kathy and Dinah were caught up in the excitement. Instead of moping around they decided to go out and look for baby-sitting jobs to help their mother, and Maxwell had already found last week's paper and had it spread open on the floor looking for a part-time job. There wasn't anything, but he wasn't discouraged. "Something'll turn up," he declared. "Somebody must need me. After all I'm not just anybody!"

"You can say that again!" I said with feeling. "But remember this has got to be secret. My father would have a fit, and so would your mother," I said to Kathy and Dinah. "So remember, mum's the word. We won't even tell Jim until we see how much we can make altogether, and then he can deduct it from Othello's price and surprise your mother."

Kathy squeezed her hands in anticipation. "She'll be surprised all right, but won't she think it's funny that his price has suddenly gone down? Everything else goes up nowadays."

"Don't worry," I said. "Jim'll think of something. He can say he's reduced for quick sale, or something like that. If your mother's got any sense, she'll just grab him and not ask any questions."

We left Kathy and Dinah feeling much happier and more hopeful. Julian went over to Holmwood Farms to offer himself for my old job, and Jim accepted him right away. Mother might have been a bit suspicious, because Julian had always reserved his Saturday mornings for hockey, but she was up to her ears in last minute sewing for Margaret, who had declared dramatically that she couldn't possibly go to Toronto and disgrace Father, looking like a provincial peasant. She planned her own wardrobe, and Mother had been constantly sewing for two weeks. She was still sewing on Saturday morning when Wallace arrived to pick Margaret up. He came roaring down our driveway in his pink, flower-covered "bug," and screeched to an ear-splitting stop, inches away from our front steps.

I was making lunch when he came flopping into the kitchen and collapsed into the nearest chair.

"Greetings, love child," he said to me, raising a limp hand.

Every time I saw him he looked hairier. I had to peer

hard at him to make sure I wasn't talking to his back.

"Greetings, goat face," I said, also raising a limp hand. "How's the painting business?"

"Dim." He slid down a notch and addressed his feet, which were now on the table. "Dismal, man, dismal! This planet is run by a conglomerate of bureaucratic nonentities with no souls."

I was contemplating going to fetch a dictionary, when we were interrupted by Margaret's shriek of welcome. She came tripping down the stairs wearing some sort of flowing artistic disaster, which she had designed herself. Mother followed with pins in her teeth, and embraced Wallace, nearly poking his eyes out.

"Lovely to see you again, dear. Now have a good time, you two, and Margaret, don't forget to remind Daddy to do his push-ups every morning, and tell him to watch his blood pressure. You know what he's like when he's producing."

Maxwell and Julian were sprawled out, reading the newspaper on the sun-porch floor, as we trooped out, each of us carrying a piece of Margaret's luggage. You would have thought she was going away for a year instead of a week.

"Aha, checking to see if you're wanted for arrest, I see," she said to Julian as she stepped over him.

"Smart!" he hissed back at her. "We're looking for jobs!"

"But you already have a job, dear," Mother reminded him.

Julian sighed heavily. "Okay, so I want two jobs. Is there any rule says a person can't have two jobs?"

"Why don't you go down to the mill and see Hamilton,"

Margaret said. "Just mention my name. He'll find you something."

"Who's Hamilton?" demanded Wallace suspiciously.

It was nice to know that Margaret wasn't perfect and slipped up occasionally. As they drove away, she was still trying to convince Wallace that Hamilton was an old family friend, with a great deal of emphasis on the "old," but Maxwell and Julian were overjoyed. They had their bicycles out and were pedaling furiously down the driveway before the dust had even settled. Mother and I went back into the kitchen and had lunch by ourselves, luxuriating in the unaccustomed peacefulness of the house.

"What's all this about Maxwell and Julian and jobs?" she asked me. "I've never seen them so anxious to work before. They must be envious of you." She smiled at me over her teacup. "You're the rich one in the family now. I'll know where to come if I'm ever short of the rent."

I gulped and must have looked slightly sick, because she hastened to reassure me. "Only kidding, dear. Don't worry. I'm glad to see you getting into the habit of saving. You're going to be glad of it when you go to college, believe me."

I thanked my lucky stars that college was a long way off. I would start worrying about my future after Mrs. Williams had Othello. Meanwhile I had enough on my plate, and it didn't help when Maxwell and Julian came back from the village and informed me that Hamilton had agreed to give them jobs during the school break on the condition that I went out with him while Margaret was away.

"Never!" I cried in alarm. "Not over my dead body!"

"He's not interested in your dead body," Maxwell informed me.

"But it's out-and-out bribery!" I protested.

"Okay, so it's bribery," said Julian with a shrug. "But it's also twenty dollars each for Maxwell and me, and that's forty dollars if you can add, which would probably buy Othello's tail and possibly a hoof thrown in for good measure."

"Do you have to be so horribly clinical?" I groaned. I felt that this was too much to ask of me, on top of giving up my bank account, but duty demanded self-sacrifice, so I steeled myself and went off to see Hamilton. I found him in the depths of the cavernous mill, shifting bags of feed from one side of the warehouse to the other. It seemed a fruitless occupation to me, but no doubt he had his reasons.

"Greetings, Hamilton," I said, sitting down on a load of fertilizer. "I hear you'll give Maxwell and Julian a job if I go out with you."

"Yup," he said, hefting a bag of feed across my head.

"All right," I said. "I'll go out with you, but I think it's only fair to warn you. Margaret's bound to hear about it in a small village like this when she gets back, and then not only will she never speak to you again, she'll probably kill us both in the bargain."

"Stop putting me on," said Hamilton, missing my head with a bag of feed by inches.

I ducked and persevered gamely. "I'm not putting you on, Hamilton. It's her hot-blooded writer's temperament that does it. You wouldn't want to be maimed for life, would you, because she's never been a very good shot?"

Hamilton moved the last sack, and came and sat down beside me. He brushed his hands on his overalls, and a powdery dust rose from him covering me in white. On top of that I started to sneeze.

"You don't like me, do you?" said Hamilton.

"Oh, Hamilton, I do!" I protested, sneezing my head off. "It's just that I'm allergic to you."

He handed me an oily rag to blow my nose on and said philosophically, "Oh, that's all right. You don't have to make excuses. I just fancied a bit of a change, that's all. But no sweat! Tell your kid brothers to report for work on Monday."

I really did like him then. I almost kissed him, but I was sneezing so badly I didn't think I was particularly desirable, so I contented myself with shaking his hand and telling him that he was terrific and I could see why Margaret was crazy about him. I fled from the mill, ecstatic with triumph. Now I had a job; Maxwell and Julian had jobs; and it turned out that even Kathy and Dinah had managed to find a cat that wanted boarding while its owners went down south for the week.

We met together and congratulated ourselves on our good start.

"At this rate," declared Julian, "we'll have Othello by the end of April."

"Oh, yes!" cried Dinah, clasping her thin little hands together in delight. "And Mommy's doing all right, too. She's got another job baking twice a week for the village bakeshop. It means she has to stay up late baking when she comes home from other jobs, but she says she can catch up on her sleep when she's got Othello." She sighed, her excitement evaporating a little. "If only we could tell her, she wouldn't have to feel so desperate."

I shook my head firmly. "I'm sorry, Dinah, but no way. She must never know. Nobody must, except Jim, and we won't tell him until we're good and ready. Anyway, with us helping, she's going to get Othello a lot sooner; then everything will be back to normal for you."

Maxwell scratched his head, looking slightly bewildered. "Isn't it funny," he said, "why grown-ups are too proud to accept money from children? When I grow up, I'm going to accept money from anybody who wants to give it to me—children included!"

Another Crisis Arises

WE HAD gotten off to a great start, but once we were back at school, things slowed down. Still we were not discouraged. There was the money from my riding lessons coming in, and Julian's Saturday morning job, and two and a half months to go before there was any danger of Mr. Jones buying Othello. With our contributions, we felt sure now that Mrs. Williams would get her bid in first, so I was really surprised to come home from school one day to find Kathy and Dinah sitting on our doorstep surrounded by our dogs, looking the picture of misery.

"Hey, what's up?" I said. "Don't tell me your mother's had more car trouble!"

Dinah shook her head woefully. "It's not that, Joanna. Kathy and I got talking together last night, and you know something—it won't end when we get Othello. It'll get worse."

"What are you talking about?" I exclaimed indignantly. "How will it? Your mother's only doing all these extra jobs so she can buy him. Once you've got him, what's the problem? Everything will be back to normal, except that you'll have a nice horse of your own."

"No, it won't," said Dinah solemnly. "It'll never be normal again, because there's something we've all forgotten—the cost of keeping a horse. Where's that money going to come from? We don't have a barn, so we'll have to board him, and you know how much that costs. Even if we did have a barn, we only have ten acres, so we'd have to buy all his feed, and then there's the extra things like vet bills, and having his hoofs trimmed." Her hands twisted together nervously in her lap. "We're going to have to live like this for the rest of our lives, if we get Othello. Mommy's going to work herself to death, and heaven knows when she'll find time to ride him. You've all been so awfully kind to try and help us, but nobody's thought about afterward. Honestly, I think it's better if we don't try and help Mommy after all."

I was so flabbergasted at this sudden change of plan, I was unable to say a word. I could only stare at Dinah, my mind churning. Why hadn't we thought about that before? We knew from experience that a horse was an expensive animal to keep. In fact, now that I thought about it, it was only after we had acquired Horse the Second that our allowances had turned to IOUs as Father became loaded down with bills for hay and oats and fresh straw.

There seemed no way out of this problem. We couldn't go on helping Mrs. Williams financially after she had Othello, because there would be no longer any way of keeping it secret, and she wouldn't accept any help openly. It seemed that Kathy and Dinah were right. Othello, that dear, mischievous charger of a horse, could only bring extended misery to the family as Mrs. Williams fought valiantly to keep abreast of the bills with her numerous jobs. But what if she were to get him anyway, without our help? I ground my fists into my forehead in an agony of frustration, wishing that once, just once, something in my life could be uncomplicated.

Maxwell and Julian came cycling down the driveway and pulled up short at the sight of us. Even the dogs were drooping, caught up in our misery, and could hardly raise a thump of their tails.

"Good grief!" exclaimed Maxwell. "It must be tapioca for dessert again!"

I looked at him in disgust. "Can't you think of anything else besides your stomach! This is far, far worse. Kathy and Dinah have decided that it's better for everybody if we don't help their mother get Othello. In fact"—I hated to say it, and the words stuck in my throat—"it would probably be better if we tried to hinder her, though heaven knows how we can do that."

Maxwell and Julian gaped at us. "You must be nuts!" exclaimed Julian. "After all that money we earned during the school break, you want to give up? What's the matter with you?"

We had to explain then, and for once in their lives they

had no answers. "How come nobody thought of that before?" said Maxwell dismally. "Dad's always saying he'll have to send Horse the Second to the glue factory if the price of feed goes up any more. Of course he's only joking," he added hastily, seeing the look of alarm on Kathy's face, "but it is true. Horses are expensive to keep."

"Have you talked to your mother about it?" Julian asked Dinah. "She must realize what it costs to keep a horse, doesn't she?"

Dinah gave a helpless shrug. "Oh, you don't know my mother. Her favorite saying is, We'll cross that bridge when we come to it, but when she crosses this bridge, it'll be too late. We'll be stuck with Othello, and that means Mommy'll have to go on working night and day to keep him, because she'll never give him up once she's got him." Her eyes brimmed with tears. "It's going to be awful whether we get him or not, because if we don't get him now, she's going to be heartbroken, she's been working so hard. But I honestly think it's better if she doesn't because she'd only be unhappy for a while, then she'd forget once he'd left Holmwood Farms. It would be like someone dying. You get over it. But if she gets him, we're all going to be miserable forever and ever, as far as I can see."

It was a horrible situation, and once again I seemed to be responsible. If I hadn't fallen off Othello, Mrs. Williams would never have met him; but neither would the riding school have come into existence, and the riding school had done wonders for Dinah and Kathy. And there again I was partially to blame; everything had been fine until I had put my big foot into it and persuaded Mrs.

Williams to ride. Before that, she had been quite content to see Kathy and Dinah enjoying themselves. Sometimes I couldn't help thinking it would be better for everybody if I stuck my head in the gas oven, except that ours was electric, so I would make a mess of that, too. For a moment, I felt utterly hopeless. I slumped down on the step beside Dinah and Kathy. "So," I groaned. "What do we do now, then?"

No one had any suggestions. If the others felt the way I did, they just wanted to find a big hole somewhere, curl up in it, and die. Even Maxwell's inventive mind failed him. We were a sorry lot, drooping all over the sun-porch steps with faces a mile long, when Margaret came tripping out of the house on her way to meet Hamilton. She had not been discovered in Toronto, as she had hoped, but some junior-assistant somebody or other at the television studios had given her a wolf whistle, and she took this as a hopeful sign. Convinced now that her future lay in the performing arts, she had decided to form an amateur theatrical group in the village, with Hamilton as her leading man. He didn't share her enthusiasm at all, but that had never deterred Margaret. She had been working on him every night for a week, and knowing the two of them, I would have put my money on Margaret every time.

"What's going on here?" she said, gingerly stepping around our slumped bodies. "Custer's last stand?"

"Oh, buzz off," I said irritably. "It's got nothing to do with you."

That was the worst thing to say to Margaret. "Everything has something to do with me," she simpered. "When you have a great need to create, then you must become a student of the world, or you'll never have any success."

"Well, bully for you," I said sourly. "You can have the world with pleasure. As far as I'm concerned, it's a mess."

That intrigued her. Instead of going on her way, she sat down in the middle of us and took over. "Now children," she said with an expansive gesture of her hands that nearly decapitated Maxwell. "Just tell Auntie Margaret your problem, and I guarantee I will solve it in two seconds flat."

Maxwell and Julian glared at her, making it quite clear that as far as they were concerned, Auntie Margaret could go and jump in the pond. I ignored her completely, but Kathy and Dinah were desperate enough to resort to any measures.

"Why don't we tell her?" said Dinah, turning to me. "It doesn't have to be a great secret now, and we don't have anything to lose. Maybe she'll think of something." They were evidently quite impressed with Margaret and her grand airs, and I was too despondent to care very much.

"Suit yourself," I said. "It doesn't matter to me, but you're wasting your time."

"We'll see about that," said Margaret, with a sniff. She dismissed the rest of us as not worth bothering with, and addressed herself to Kathy and Dinah. "You know what I do when I have a problem?" she said, smiling sweetly at them. "I pretend the problem is two acts of a three-act play, so all I have to do is think up the last act and there's the solution to the problem. It's much easier that way, because you can always think of endings to plays or books, but your own problems always seem insoluble. It's just a different approach, that's all, but it makes all the difference."

"Oh, sure," I said bitterly. "And what if the last act consists of everybody committing suicide on the sun-porch steps, like in Hamlet?" But nobody was listening to me. Kathy and Dinah were already spilling out their sorry tale of woe, and soon Margaret had the whole story.

"Hmm!" she said, pursing up her lips. "Hah!"

"What kind of a last act is that?" I wanted to know; but she only gave me her lofty look and said archly, "If you will only be quiet for five minutes, I will let you know the prognosis." Since none of us was sure what she was talking about, we couldn't argue with her. We sat in sullen silence long enough for me to wonder if Margaret had gone into a trance when she suddenly said, "Aha!"

"You're beginning to sound more like Hamilton every day," I complained. "Your vocabulary is getting more and more limited."

"Keep out of this, Joanna," she snarled at me aside, then turned back to Kathy and Dinah with a radiant smile on her face. "There is only one solution," she burbled at them. "They must fall in love."

We gaped at her with sick expressions on our faces. "Who must fall in love?" I exploded. "What kind of a solution is that?"

"It's the only solution," she declared, supremely confident in her ability to handle world affairs. "Kathy and Dinah, Mr. Holmes must fall in love with your mother. Once he's in love with her, he'll do anything she asks. Then she only has to tell him that she doesn't want him to sell Othello, and her slightest wish will be his command. Othello can stay on at the riding school; your mother can ride him whenever she pleases; and two lonely people will bring joy to each other's lives. Now what could be a better last act than that?"

"Yuck!" said Maxwell.

"Excuse me while I throw up," said Julian.

I hadn't any words at all, and it was Kathy who surprised us all by saying, starry-eyed, "Oh, Margaret, do you really think Mr. Holmes might fall in love with Mommy? I really like him, and if we have to have another father I'd rather it was him than anybody. We could live in that lovely house and not only Othello but all the horses would belong to us. Wouldn't that be fantastic?"

"Now wait! Just a minute!" I cried, feeling that things were getting out of hand. "You don't make people fall in love with each other, Kathy. You don't arrange things like that." I glared at Margaret accusingly. "That's crazy!"

"No, it isn't," she replied airily. "It happens all the time. Put two lonely people in the right atmosphere at the right time, and the next thing you know—bingo!—they're in love. Your mother is a very attractive woman, Kathy, and since old Mr. Holmes and John have left the big house, Mr. Holmes is a very lonely man. You told me that yourself, Joanna, so there's your solution." She stood up as Hamilton's truck turned into our driveway. "I have to go now, children. Think about it, and if you need any more advice, just come and see Auntie Margaret."

We watched, glassy-eyed, as she jumped into the truck beside Hamilton, giving us a queenly wave as they drove off.

Dinah was the first one to find her voice. "Do you think it might work?" she said incredulously.

"You, too!" I turned on her in amazement. "Oh, Dinah, you can't take Margaret seriously. She always lives in a romantic, make-believe world. Those sort of things don't happen in real life, you know that."

"I don't see why it couldn't," said Kathy earnestly. "Daddy met somebody he liked better than Mommy, so I don't see why she can't meet somebody she likes better than Daddy, particularly if he's rich and owns Othello."

Julian, Maxwell, and I looked at each other in despair. "That Margaret!" was Maxwell's disgusted comment. "Someone should have put her in boiling oil when she was a baby. I'm going skating. I don't know anything about that yucky love stuff. Coming, Julian?"

Julian glanced at Dinah, but she was too absorbed in her thoughts to pay any attention to him. "Might as well, I s'pose," he said, disgruntled. "We can talk about it later when you come to your senses."

They went off scowling and scuffing the last traces of snow on the path with their heels. Left alone with Dinah and Kathy, I didn't know what to do. I could tell they were completely bewitched by Margaret's idea, and if I hadn't felt so responsible, I would gladly have walked off, too, and washed my hands of the whole affair.

Kathy was looking at me, all excited. "Joanna, couldn't we try it, just to see what happens? I mean, Mommy's never met Mr. Holmes, and it might just work. Couldn't you get your mother to ask them to dinner together, or something? She knows both of them, and Mommy looks really super when she's dressed up—you've no idea. Oh, Joanna, couldn't you please? If it doesn't work, it doesn't, but at least we could try!"

They were ganging up on me now. Dinah, the more sensible of the two, said solemnly, "They needn't necessarily get married, but if they could become friends, Mommy might talk to him about Othello, and then maybe he wouldn't sell him after all. It would solve everything, Joanna. It really would!"

What could I do? I didn't have any alternative suggestions to offer, and I was so anxious to find a solution to the problem I had created, I even began to get a little bit excited myself. But I didn't want to get into any more trouble, and since it was Margaret's idea, I decided to dump the whole thing back in her lap. When she came back from her date, I managed to get her alone, and told her that she had Kathy and Dinah all worked up, and now they wanted me to arrange a dinner meeting without making anyone suspicious, and as far as I could see, that was impossible. "Auntie Margaret," I said sourly, "you got us into this mess. Now kindly get us out of it, and good luck!"

"No problem," she said with a shrug. "Just leave it to me. My birthday's on Saturday, so I'll just tell Mother I want to have an adult party for a change. She can come and Daddy, and I'll ask Mr. Holmes, Mrs. Williams, and Hamilton. They're just about all the adults I know, so she won't be suspicious. You kids can make yourselves scarce."

I closed my eyes as my heart sank. "Not Hamilton, Margaret," I begged her. "He just doesn't fit! I thought you said an adult party."

"Well, Hamilton's an adult!" she retorted indignantly. "He certainly isn't a child!"

I had to agree with her that Hamilton was in a category all of his own, but he still didn't seem to fit in any dinner party with Mr. Holmes and Mrs. Williams.

Margaret disagreed with me strongly. "He's a very romantic person when you get to know him," she told me coldly. "In fact Hamilton and I will set the mood for the party, so don't talk about something you know nothing about. And if you want me to take care of things, let me take care of them and don't interfere. Okay?"

"Okay," I said, thoroughly cowed by her imperious manner. I only hoped, as I slunk out of the room, that Auntie Margaret knew what she was doing. One thing was certain; she couldn't have any worse luck than I'd been having, and as far as I could see that was the only cheerful note in the whole sorry business.

Auntie Margaret Goofs

ONCE AGAIN I had to give Margaret credit. She might be a pain in the neck, but she knew how to get her own way. My parents were so flattered to be asked to her birthday party instead of the usual teen-age crowd that Mother went all out to plan the most elegant dinner imaginable; and Mrs. Williams was tickled pink to accept the invitation, because she never had a chance to go out anywhere these days. All we had to do now was to wait for the weekend to ask Mr. Holmes, and our plan would be complete. Dinah and Kathy were very excited. We didn't breathe to anyone a word of what we had in mind; even Mrs. Williams didn't know Mr. Holmes was coming in case she got suspicious of our intentions. We went around with our fingers crossed furiously, and couldn't wait for Saturday to come.

Since Mother and Margaret were so busy, I said I would go over to Holmwood House after my Saturday-morning riding lesson, and ask Mr. Holmes personally. Kathy and Dinah volunteered to come with me. As we walked over to the house, they told me of their plans to make their mother look so glamorous, no one could resist her.

"She has this tight black sweater," Dinah told me, her eyes shining in anticipation, "and this long red skirt, and she wears it with big gold earrings. She looks terrific, almost like a gypsy, but at the same time she looks ladylike, if you know what I mean. I expect men like that, don't you? It must be very exciting to them."

I had to admit that I didn't have much experience in such matters. John Holmes was the only boyfriend I had ever had in my life, and his pet name for me was Funny Face.

"We're going to do her hair," said Kathy, skipping along beside me. "We've got this terrific new style out of a magazine, and as soon as she comes home this afternoon, we're going to wash it and set it the way the book says. She's going to look like a model when we've finished with her."

"Isn't she home this morning?" I asked.

Kathy pulled a face. "No, she went out before we got up. Some stupid new cleaning job. She does so many now we can't keep track of them, but she left a note saying she'd be back for lunch, so we've got all afternoon to work on her." She grinned at me impishly. "Oh, Joanna, this is fun, isn't it? Do you think Mr. Holmes will like her?"

"He likes you two well enough, Tweedledum and

Tweedledee," I said, smiling, "so I don't see why not. They both like horses, so they have that in common. We'll just have to hope for the best."

We entered Holmwood House by the back door. All Jim's lady riders came back to the kitchen for coffee after their lessons, and Mrs. Bentley was used now to people trooping in without knocking. In fact she had told me she enjoyed the company, even though it meant cleaning the floor two or three times a week. It was better than the old days when the house was spotless but empty from Monday to Friday. She was perched on a stepladder by the basement steps, washing the walls, as we filed in the door.

"Watch your muddy feet, children," she called down to us. "It's spring-cleaning day today. Did you want to see Mr. Holmes, Joanna? He only just got up, because he was late last night—some convention or other in the city. He's having breakfast in the morning room."

We dutifully unshod ourselves of our riding boots, and made our way across the large bright kitchen to the morning-room annex, which was closed off with louvered doors. We were so intent on our errand, we did not notice we were not alone in the kitchen, until a cheery voice said, "Well, Kathy and Dinah, what are you doing here?" We spun around startled out of our wits just in time to see Mrs. Williams' head emerge from the oven, which she had been busy cleaning. I thought my eyes were playing tricks on me. She had her hair scraped back so tightly under a bandanna that not a trace of it showed, and she wore rubber gloves and a huge working apron over an old blouse and slacks. To top off this glamorous sight, there was a smudge of oven grease on her chin, and her face was shiny and red with exertion.

Kathy and Dinah let out simultaneous gasps of horror. "Mommy!" gasped Kathy. "You can't work here! Not *here*!"

"Oh, come off it, Kathy!" Mrs. Williams sat back on the heels of her old sneakers, and looked at her younger daughter with disapproval. "Aren't you being a bit silly about this? Mrs. Bentley told me she was looking for help with the spring cleaning, so I volunteered. What's so terrible about that?"

If she only knew! I could only hope that Mr. Holmes never came into the kitchen, but even as I tried to console myself with the thought that it was very unlikely, out of the corner of my eye, I saw the louvered doors swing inward and Mr. Holmes poked his head around. "Why, hello Joanna," he said rather absentmindedly. He still had the morning paper in his hand, and his glasses on his nose. "Have you seen Mrs. Bentley anywhere about?"

I heard strangled noises behind me, and I knew what had happened. Kathy and Dinah, acting on impulse, had thrust their mother back into the oven, and she was protesting vehemently.

"Yes, Mr. Holmes, she's out by the basement steps," I said, baring my teeth at him in a ghastly attempt at a smile. I don't know why I hoped he would ignore the muffled explosions of wrath behind me as Kathy and Dinah practically sat on their mother, or that part of her that was protruding, in an effort to keep her hidden, but hope I did. I had a desperate thought that if I kept on chattering away and acting naturally as though nothing out of the ordinary were going on, he might think he was having hallucinations after his late night and go back to bed. Unfortunately it didn't work. Mrs. Williams burst out of the confining oven, nearly toppling Kathy and Dinah over backward. Her bandanna was askew, her face scarlet and even more smudged. Hands on hips, she stood up full of righteous indignation and declared, "What on earth do you two think you're doing?"

I saw Mr. Holmes's eyes pop. He took off his glasses and blinked, and now I think he did think he was having hallucinations, but it was too late. Mrs. Williams had seen him. You would have thought she would have had the grace to be embarrassed, but not a bit of it. "Oh, you must be Mr. Holmes," she said, giving him a charming smile through all that grease, for all the world as though she were at a tea party at Buckingham Palace. "I'm so glad to meet you. Kathy and Dinah have told me so much about you." While we watched in utter horror, she went forward and held out her rubber-gloved hand. "I hope you'll forgive my daughters larking around. They're impossible little teases, at times."

"Why, yes—yes, of course." Mr. Holmes seemed slightly bemused, and I didn't blame him. "You must be Mrs. Williams." As an afterthought, he remembered his manners, and shook her wet rubber hand, which must have felt like a dead fish. "I—I'm very pleased to meet you."

I wanted the floor to open and swallow me up, and I'm sure Kathy and Dinah did, too. Fortunately for all of us, Mrs. Bentley chose that moment to come into the kitchen to refill her bucket of water. "Oh, Mr. Holmes," she said, "do you know Mrs. Williams? She's helping me with the spring cleaning."

"Yes—yes, I can see that. Yes—well we've just met." He looked rather confused, poor man, and I think he was glad of an excuse to escape. "I just wanted to let you know, Mrs. Bentley, that I won't be home for supper tonight. I'm taking some people from the convention out to dinner. A late lunch will do around two o'clock." He was practically backing into the morning room as he spoke, nodding his head and giving us forced little smiles. "Very nice to have met you, Mrs. Williams. See you around, Tweedledum, Tweedledee."

The louvered doors swung shut behind him, and Mrs. Williams said, "So that's your Mr. Holmes, is it? He seems very nice. Now what was all that carrying on about? Really, you children are terrible at times!"

"Didn't you want to see Mr. Holmes?" Mrs. Bentley asked me.

"It doesn't matter," I said in a flat voice. "It wasn't very important."

Outside again, Kathy, Dinah, and I looked at each other in despair. "She ruined it!" cried Kathy almost in tears. "Did you see the way he looked at her, and she had to make him shake hands, too! I bet he goes straight up to the bathroom and scrubs his hands for half an hour!"

"He couldn't have come anyway," I said flatly. "He was going out." I felt too dispirited to care much anymore. "We'd better go and tell Auntie Margaret to keep her wonderful advice to herself in future."

She was busy making a table decoration out of candles and dried flowers when we found her and broke the news. For a moment she was taken off stride, but only for a moment. "Well," she said with a sigh, "it can't be helped. We'll have to use this dinner party as a sort of dress rehearsal for the next one."

"What next one?" I almost shrieked at her. "Are you out of your mind? You don't think anything's going to come of it now, do you? I've never seen anyone look so awful in my life as she did when she came out of the oven!"

"Oh, don't exaggerate!" said Margaret, and she had the nerve to add, "That's your trouble. You overdramatize everything. We'll have another dinner party in two-weeks time, and then he'll have forgotten all about it. And next time we'll ask him a week ahead of time, so that we'll be sure he comes."

I put my head in my hands and groaned. "Margaret, even if that were true, what excuse are you going to give Mother for wanting another party so soon? They cost money, you know."

She shrugged and went back to her flower arranging. "I'll think of something. I'll tell Mother it's Hamilton's birthday."

"Is it Hamilton's birthday?" I asked suspiciously.

"No," said Margaret. "His birthday's in July, but what's three months here or there? He'll understand. He can have another one in July if he wants. I'll take care of everything, so just stop worrying."

"Oh sure!" I said, and I could hardly be blamed if I

sounded slightly bitter. "Leave everything to Auntie Margaret, and it'll all come up roses. Big deal!"

But we didn't really have much say in the matter. Now Margaret had taken over, we were putty in her hands, and Kathy and Dinah, little optimists that they were, began to be hopeful again.

"Maybe she's right," said Dinah. "Mr. Holmes probably had his mind on the convention anyway, and men don't remember things the way women do. When he sees her all dressed up, he'll never think about the first time."

I don't know where she became such an expert on men all of a sudden, but I kept out of it. It was Margaret's baby now, not mine. I ended up taking Mr. Holmes's place at dinner, and in spite of my disappointment I had to admit it was a success. Mother was a wonderful cook, and we ate by candlelight with soft music playing. Mrs. Williams looked lovely, and I could only hope that the real thing would be half as successful as the dress rehearsal. Even Hamilton wore a suit, smelled of after-shave lotion instead of malt, and astounded me by making one or two intelligent remarks about the price of grain.

In fact it was so successful, that after our guests had gone and we were sitting around having a nightcap, Father said, "We should do this more often. Country living tends to make one slipshod. I'm sorry Jack Holmes couldn't come. I feel we owe him something after all the help he's given Joanna."

That was Margaret's cue. She didn't even have to mention Hamilton's birthday. "Well let's have another one for Mr. Holmes in a couple of weeks," she suggested blithely, "before the table decorations get too dusty. We can ask him a week ahead of time, this time, so he can make his arrangements accordingly."

"Well, I don't know, dear," said Mother. "That's rather soon isn't it?"

"No, it isn't. If we wait much longer the hot weather will be here, and nobody'll want to eat inside. There's nothing elegant about a barbecue. Anybody who's anybody does their entertaining at this time of the year."

Mother couldn't argue with that since we didn't really know anybody who was anybody, except perhaps Mr. Holmes, and since this dinner would be for him, she wanted to do it right. So a date two weeks ahead was decided upon, and I didn't know whether to become hopeful again or not, so I just stayed neutral.

When next Saturday came around, I gave my usual morning lesson, and Mr. Holmes came over to watch as he often did. I was determined to waylay him as soon as the lesson was over and give him the invitation for next weekend, so there would be no more mix-ups. The lesson was going on a bit longer than usual, because Polly Jones had taken it into her head that she wanted to try out Othello in case they bought him. She was a bit scared of him, and sensing this, he had been in a mischievous mood all through the lesson, spooking at nothing, prancing about like a prima donna, and running out of all the jumps. I kept telling Polly to relax, sit deep in the saddle, and get her knees on him tight. I had to do my job as a teacher, even though I was secretly rather glad that Polly couldn't handle him, but I couldn't get through to her. In the end

Mr. Holmes stepped into the ring and took over from me.

"You've got a good horse there, Polly," he said. "Now show him who's boss. He's playing with you. Take that jump again, and if he runs out, give him a good one with the crop. Let him know who's in charge. He'll soon get the idea."

Othello swerved again, and Polly gave him a little tickle on his neck. "Harder!" yelled Mr. Holmes. "Really let him have it!"

Getting braver, Polly landed a sharp one on his flank. Othello, startled, reared, and Polly, getting into the spirit of the thing, gave him two sharp slaps across his neck and sawed on his bit to bring him into line. Even I had to admit it was a spunky performance.

"That's better," Mr. Holmes called out in approval. "Now you're getting the idea. Don't let him get away with anything. Give him the crop hard, and don't be scared of using it. He has to learn."

We were all so fascinated watching Polly bring that big horse into line that we hadn't noticed Mrs. Williams come in. It was one of the few mornings she hadn't any cleaning jobs, and she had come to pick up Kathy and Dinah, who were riding Kelp and Spirit in the lesson. The first intimation we had of her presence was her clear English voice floating across the arena.

"What are you doing to that horse? Are you trying to break his spirit?"

I could see she was livid. She strode up to Mr. Holmes and really let him have it. "Is this the way you give lessons, beating a horse into submission, and you call yourself a teacher? A lovely gentle horse like Othello! That isn't my idea of teaching riding, not using brute force!"

If Mr. Holmes had been taken aback when he met her in the kitchen it was nothing to the way he looked now. He just stared at her for a moment, wondering no doubt if she was real, and one of the younger girls started to giggle. That brought him back to his senses, and he said with immense dignity, I thought, "I appreciate your taking an interest, Mrs. Williams, but I can assure you I know what I'm doing. To use a crop on a disobedient horse is not using brute force, any more than spanking your children if they disobey you."

Mrs. Williams had a blind spot where Othello was concerned. She didn't seem to notice any of us. She said coldly to Mr. Holmes, "For your information, Mr. Holmes, I have never found it necessary to spank my children when they disobey me. I reason with them, just as I reason with Othello, I can assure you."

I don't know how it would have ended, because at that moment Kathy suddenly let out a cry that was half hysterical, half sobbing, "Mommy, stop it, stop it! You're ruining everything! Stop it!"

Now she was the center of attention as we all turned to stare at her. Her face turned a bright red. She dropped Kelp's reins and ran from the arena. I didn't know what to do, so I ran after her, but she was already running across the fields toward our place. Behind me I could hear Dinah running and calling. Kathy vaulted the fence into our yard, with us hard on her heels, and headed for our barn. Horse the Second and Tangles were out in the field. When we finally caught up with her, she was banging her fists against the stall partition, sobbing wildly. We tried to comfort her, without success, and we did not notice Mrs. Williams come in behind us. She pushed us aside and knelt down beside Kathy. "What is it dear? What's the matter? Tell me."

Kathy turned to her mother, her face blotched and red with crying. "You spoilt it all!" she wailed. "You spoil everything! We wanted him to like you. We were going to ask you both to dinner next week so he would like you, and you have to yell at him like that, and you have to let him see you looking ugly and greasy, and now he'll hate you, and it's just no good! You ruin everything, and we're only trying to help you!"

Mrs. Williams turned slowly to Dinah and me. Her face was so pale I thought she was in shock. "What's she talking about, Joanna?" she asked me in a shaky voice. "Do you know?"

There seemed to be no way to keep it from her any longer, so between us Dinah and I told her everything—how we had all tried to help her get Othello, and then how afraid Kathy and Dinah had been that it wouldn't work out if she did get him. Finally we told her Margaret's plan. I didn't know what to expect. I thought she might be angry or laugh and call us ridiculous, but she did neither. She turned away and went to the door of the barn, standing there so long, looking out, that we began to get worried.

"Mommy," ventured Dinah timidly. "Are you very mad?"

"No, dear." She turned around and gave us a gentle, sad smile. "I'm not mad at all. I'm ashamed." She put her arm around Dinah, and pulled Kathy to her feet. "I've been a selfish, rotten mother, and you've every right to be mad at me. I had no right to put myself first and ignore you like this. I had no idea you were so unhappy."

She got out a handerchief and wiped Kathy's tears away. "Of course I love Othello, but you two are more important to me than anything in the world. You believe that, don't you?"

Kathy sniffed and nodded. "What are you going to do now then, Mommy?"

"We're going home," she told them. "I'm going to make a nice lunch, and afterward I'm going to clean our house from top to bottom, and ours is the only house I'm going to clean from now on. There'll be no more extra jobs after this."

"No more selling cosmetics or baking pies?" asked Kathy hopefully.

"No, dear, no more of that, either. I was getting tired of it anyway. It was more fun being a full-time mother."

"But what about Othello?"

A wistful smile hovered on her face, but then she said heartily, "He was a dream, dear. Everyone has to have a dream now and then, so long as it doesn't get out of hand. Come on, what do you want for lunch? Macaroni and cheese, or spaghetti?"

They had already forgotten me. I watched them walk away with their arms around each other, and I knew I didn't belong there anyway. This was their private time, which outsiders couldn't share. Instead I walked into the field and waited for Horse the Second and Tangles to come running up to me, butting and pummeling their way through my pockets. Tangles was the only lamb I knew who liked sugar.

"Well," I told them philosophically, "we seem to have made a lovely mess of everything again. Three cheers for us."

Then I went back to the house to tell Margaret that she might as well call off her dinner party because under the circumstances I didn't think somehow that it would be a great success.

Father Gets into the Act

MY FAMILY were all at lunch. I couldn't have felt less like eating, but it was easier to flop down at the table than to drag myself up to my room.

"Well?" queried Margaret brightly. "Did you ask him?"

"No," I said. "There's no point now. Mrs. Williams knows everything, and as for Mr. Holmes, if they were the last two people left on earth, I doubt if he'd speak to her."

Of course, having given away that much, my parents had to be told the whole story. I half hoped my father would get mad, because I was spoiling for a good fight to unleash some of my frustration, but unpredictable as always, he started to laugh. He slapped his thigh and guffawed.

"My God!" he said. "You kids really take the cake! You're so devious, you ought to be in politics."

We didn't think it was so funny. We hunched over our soup bowls and glared at him. "It was that yucky love stuff that ruined it all," Maxwell accused Margaret. "Why didn't you keep out of it?"

"Look who's talking!" cried Margaret indignantly. "I didn't see you coming up with any bright solutions when you asked for my help. And it was you lot who botched up this dinner business, not me. Good grief, you can't even give somebody a little thing like an invitation without messing everything up. You should get the Disaster of the Year award, you lot!"

"Thanks a lot, Auntie Margaret," I growled. "Ann Landers certainly doesn't have to worry about you for competition—that's for sure!"

"Now that's enough!" Mother banged the soup ladle on the table to restore order. "I've no doubt you meant well and you did your best, but I wish you would all learn to mind your own business. All you've done, as far as I can see, is cause a lot of trouble for Mrs. Williams and her family, and achieved nothing." She cast a look of disapproval at Father who was still chuckling to himself. "That poor woman. I must admit I didn't think she was a very good mother, but I have to take that back now. What a disappointment for her, after she's worked so hard, poor thing. I don't suppose she's had a very easy life. I wish there was something we could do for her."

"Oh, no!" I sat bolt upright and fixed her with a steely eye. "Don't you start! That's how it all begins, with a harmless little remark, and next thing you're in it up to your neck. We're supposed to be minding our own business, remember?" I glared at my mother and slumped back over my soup bowl, viciously stirring alphabet noodles into a whirlpool with my spoon.

Father leaned over the table and wagged a finger at me. "Ah, yes, Joanna, but the trouble with your schemes is that you have no organization. You get a wild idea and plunge right in without taking any time to think things out logically. You also have a very unfortunate habit of being underhand and sly, which, God knows, you don't get from me. Now if this plan of yours had been managed properly from the start, it's quite possible Mrs. Williams would have gotten her horse and arrangements made to keep it without too much financial embarrassment."

I jerked my head up and looked to see if he was joking, but he was serious. "You're kidding!" I said.

"Not at all." He leaned back in his chair and folded his arms. "It's just a question of logical thinking. Now what is the most important problem at the moment? Keeping the horse after it has been acquired, I believe."

"Well, I suppose so," I admitted, "but—"

"Never mind the buts, Joanna. One thing at a time. Mrs. Williams can't afford to board this horse, and she doesn't have a barn of her own, so what is the logical thing to do? Look for a friend who already has a barn with one stall standing empty, and three horse-loving youngsters who would willingly board said horse for nothing, provided they could ride it sometimes."

"Like us, you mean!" Maxwell let out a war whoop. "Gee, Dad, how come we didn't think of that?"

"Because you're not logical," said my father. "And I don't understand why you have to be so sly about everything. If you had come to me in the first place—"

I sighed. "You would have told us we were nuts," I said, knowing my father only too well. The only reason he was interested now was because we had failed miserably. "Okay, Daddy, you've solved the problem of where to keep the horse, but what about feeding him and his vet bills and things?"

My father pursed up his lips. "Well, of course, the beast would have to be fed, I grant you, but that ten acres could be put out to grass, and the small amount of money that would have to be forked out to supplement the feed in the winter wouldn't be more than the lady is already paying for riding lessons now, which, I might add, she wouldn't need if the horse belonged to her. And as for vet bills, really, Joanna! You're going out with a young fellow who's attending veterinary college. Surely you can use what feminine wiles you have to get around that little problem."

Now it was my mother's turn to laugh. "You're dreadful," she said to my father. "You're worse than the children. I don't know how you can say they don't take after you, because they certainly don't take after me."

I looked at my father with grudging admiration. "All right, Daddy," I said. "That's another problem solved, What to do with Othello after she's got him. But she hasn't got him, so what about that? She made it quite clear that she isn't going to do any more extra jobs, so it's really putting the cart before the horse this time, isn't it?"

"How much money has she got?" asked my father.

I did a quick mental calculation. "Well, she had about nine hundred dollars in her bank when her car conked out, and that cost her four hundred dollars, but with all the work she's been doing lately I bet she's back to nine hundred dollars again, but that's nowhere near enough. She needs another six hundred dollars before the middle of June. Mr. Jones won't be buying Othello before then, because he has to go to Europe on a business trip. But I bet he does as soon as he comes back; otherwise Polly wouldn't be interested in learning how to ride Othello."

Father twined his fingers together and used them to prop up his chin. "Hmm!" he said. "Six hundred dollars, eh? We must think about that."

"Must we?" I begged him. "Can't we just leave it now, Daddy, and admit that we're beaten?"

My father looked right through me, and I doubt if he even heard, but it was Margaret who said, "She wouldn't think it was charity if she was involved in some way and we all had fun together, would she?"

"What are you thinking about, dear?" asked Mother curiously.

"Amateur dramatics," said Margaret. "I've been trying to get Hamilton interested, but I need more support. If Daddy and I between us wrote a play, and we could find some place to put it on, and if we could get a hundred people to come for three nights at two dollars apiece, there's your six hundred dollars for you right there, and I'd get my company launched in the bargain."

I contorted my face into a fearful grimace. "Oh, look who's being logical now—Auntie Margaret. Don't you know that a hall costs a small fortune to rent? And what company are you talking about?"

"You," she said loftily. "All of you. Beggars can't be

choosers. I've almost got Hamilton sold on the idea, anyway, and I bet Mrs. Williams can act, with that lovely clear voice of hers. All I need is a chance to get off the ground, and from then on, it'll be plain sailing."

"If you want to get off the ground, a hot-air balloon would be a lot less complicated, because there's a lot of hot air floating around here, free," I said, scowling at her. I was suddenly very tired. I had done so much scheming and planning over the past few months, all to no avail, that I just felt too weary to get involved in some other harebrained idea which, even with the blessing of my parents, was sure to end in more heartbreak for everybody.

"I'm going out," I announced, getting up from the table. "I need some fresh air."

"Are you feeling all right, dear?" asked Mother.

"I'm feeling fine," I assured her. "I just have this sudden mad desire to become a recluse and not talk to anybody except squirrels and groundhogs."

I put on my boots and sloshed across the muddy yard and through the furrows in the fields, where rivulets of melting snow created numerous lakes and ponds, reflecting fluffy clouds in a Dresden-blue sky. I was suffering from a bad case of anticlimax blues. Now that veterinary school was out, John was spending a holiday with his grandfather in Florida, and I wished I could have been with him, sunning myself under palm trees on some beautiful silvery beach, with the surf lulling me to sleep. But that was wishful thinking. Instead of the sea, I was standing in mud up to my ankles, and Holmwood Farms stretched away below me, the barns and buildings almost indecently white against the dreary background of melting snow and ice. I continued down to the paddocks with no particular purpose in mind, except that I knew I would find the presence of horses comforting. I opened the door to the big barn and almost bumped into Jim coming out.

"Hey, what a long face!" he said. "Are you missing your boyfriend?"

"Among other things," I said. "Did you hear about Mrs. Williams telling Mr. Holmes off?"

He laughed. "Yes, he told me. He's thinking of putting a sign up on the barn saying, 'Parents Keep Out.' "

I groaned. "He was mad then, eh?"

"No, not mad. He was more amused than anything. It's not the first time a doting mother has told him she knows more than he does. I wouldn't worry about it, sweetheart." He leaned against the tack-room door, and cocked an eyebrow at me. "You look as if you could use a little treat. I've got half an hour to spare, so how about you and me taking Queenie into the arena and seeing if you've forgotten how to ride a good horse?"

"Queenie!" I stared at him in disbelief, but the more I thought about it, it didn't seem such a wild idea after all. I had begun riding again on Horse because by no stretch of the imagination could you call her high-spirited, and there was no danger of her throwing me; yet, on the other hand, to make her go at all, I had really had to work hard, and my back hadn't suffered at all. It was weeks now since I had felt a twinge, and I was suddenly full of confidence that I could handle Queenie again.

"Oh, Jim," I said, getting that nervous tingling feeling again that I used to get before shows. "Do you think I could?"

"I don't see why not," he said. "Mr. Holmes was discussing it with your father the other day and apparently your back's mending nicely. We'll have to give the jumps a miss for a while of course, but you have to start again sometime. Besides," he added, taking my arm and leading me to her stall, "you look so down, you need something to put the sparkle back in your eyes."

So, after months and months, I rode Queenie again with Jim putting us through our paces, just like the old days. I walked, trotted, and cantered her, and after dear old Horse, it was a breeze. I hadn't forgotten how to ride her, after all. Jim even put up the six-inch cavalletti in a row, and I trotted her over those. Next time it would be higher, and I would eventually get back to jumping. I was in my own personal heaven again. On the way home, I didn't even notice the mud, only the first meadow larks skimming the fields and the thin, high call of the killdeers heralding spring. It was a lovely world again. John could have his golden beaches and his palm trees. I was back with Queenie, and I was happy.

I couldn't wait to tell somebody, but when I got into the kitchen, there were Margaret, Julian, and Maxwell all in a huddle at the table. As soon as they saw me, they all started talking at once.

"It's all settled. Margaret and Dad have got the craziest idea for a play. It's wild!"

"We're going to call it 'Mother Wants a Horse,' and

Julian and I are going to be the horse. We're going to make a papier-mâché head and put a blanket over us, and I'm going to be the back legs and Julian's going to be the front. It's going to be crazy!"

"We're going to use our old barn for the theater. We won't have to rent a hall, and it won't cost us anything."

"Hey, wait a minute!" I protested, putting my hands over my ears. "Am I hearing right? You're going to put on a play in our old barn? But it's only a shell. Have you forgotten that we stripped it to make the new barn for Horse?"

Margaret gave a long-suffering sigh. "We're not stupid, Joanna. The foundations are still there, and that'll be the auditorium with a bit of cleaning up. And the end where the hayloft was, which you didn't pull down, that'll be the stage when we're finished with it. It still has a roof and floorboards, and the cow shed at the back will be the dressing rooms. There won't be any curtains or anything. It'll be a very modern play with bits of movable scenery here and there to give effect. Daddy's out there now looking it over, and Mother's phoning up Grandma to see if she can get the minister to lend her a hundred folding chairs from the church hall for a good cause."

"Do you think Mrs. Williams is a good cause?" I said. "And what's all this about the play being called 'Mother Wants a Horse'?"

Margaret chuckled to herself. "That's the great part—Mrs. Williams gave us the idea. But we're going to do it so that it's a sort of Victorian melodrama in a modern setting. We're going to have the heroine a poor widow with two children who falls in love with a horse owned by the villain, complete with black moustache, cloak, and everything. The villain wants to sell the horse, but of course the poor widow can't afford to buy it. He wants to marry her anyway, but she says, 'No, no, a thousand times, no, I'd rather rob banks than say yes.' So she tries every possible way to make money, like robbing banks and forging checks and gambling, but nothing comes off because she's the goody, you see, and she's always giving it away. In the end she's forced to marry the villain, but she isn't disheartened because she has a plan up her sleeve. As soon as the villain says, chuckling slyly, 'With all my worldly goods, I thee endow,' the two children lead in the horse, which is now legally hers, and they all jump on his back and gallop away into the sunset, with Mother playing 'Just a Song at Twilight' on her violin behind the scenery."

"Isn't it great?" whooped Maxwell, turning a handspring and missing Blob by inches. "Can't you just see it?"

"All those nutty characters," chortled Julian. "We're going to have a ball! Dad and Margaret are going to start writing it tonight after supper."

I was truly speechless for a while; then I said, "Are you serious?"

"Of course, we're serious," said Margaret impatiently. "Don't you have any imagination, Joanna? It's going to be the most hilarious thing you ever saw."

"Well, I agree with you there," I said with feeling. "But you can't make Mr. Holmes out to be a villain. That's the last thing he is, and he's liable to sue you for libel."

Margaret made a face. "Oh, come off it, Joanna. It's

not really meant to be Mrs. Williams and Mr. Holmes. It's just that we got the idea from her—that's all."

"Well it sounds very much like her to me," I said sourly, "with two daughters, and wanting a horse so much she'll do anything to get it, so naturally Mr. Holmes will think the villain is supposed to be him, especially after her run-in with him in the arena this morning. He's going to be terribly hurt, after he's been so nice to us."

"He doesn't know Mrs. Williams wants Othello," Julian reminded me.

"No," I said, "but I presume she's going to play herself in the play, so he'll soon get the idea, particularly when she buys Othello with the money from the play. I doubt if he'll ever speak to us again."

Margaret threw up her hands in despair. "Can't you ever be constructive, Joanna? Must you always be the world's worst pessimist? I suppose you're afraid he'll be so offended, he'll get someone else to ride Queenie. Well, I've got news for you, little sister. Mr. Holmes isn't interested in local drama groups. He comes down here on Friday nights just to be with his horses, not to socialize, you know that. If he wants theater, he can go to the best there is in the city. He isn't about to spend his time patronizing amateur theatricals, so stop being so selfish, and think of someone else besides you and your precious Queenie for a change."

I thought that was really the limit, calling me selfish after I had done so much to try and help Mrs. Williams get Othello. I felt like blowing my top, but I couldn't be bothered. All I had wanted to do was tell someone about me and Queenie, but under the circumstances I thought that had better wait, too.

"You're going to have to help, you know," Maxwell told me, sternly. "Everyone's got to pitch in. If you're not acting, you'll have to sell programs or shift scenery or something. Dad says it has to be a real communal effort."

"Oh, does he?" I said. "I suppose he's going to play the villain. Well, it should come naturally to him."

"No, I'm going to write that part especially for Hamilton," Margaret told me proudly. "Dad's going to direct. It's always been a secret ambition of his to direct a play."

"Oh, lovely!" I groaned. "Hamilton as leading man, and Dad as director! Today the cow barn, tomorrow Broadway! I don't believe it!"

I went upstairs and considered drawing out my bank account for a one-way ticket to Australia. In the end I decided that I couldn't escape my family even if I went to the moon. Somehow they would reach out and get me, so if I couldn't beat them I had better join them, and try to inject a bit of sanity into the proceedings if such a thing were possible.

Mother Wants a Horse

ONE THING about Father, when he embarked on any project, his enthusiasm was such that it swept away all obstacles in its path. Soon all of us, myself included, were totally involved in the play that was to launch Margaret in her new career, and acquire Othello all in one fell swoop. I hadn't been there when they approached Mrs. Williams, purposely making myself as scarce as possible, but I heard afterward from Margaret that she had burst into tears.

"I'm not surprised," I said. "I imagine it would have that effect on some people."

Margaret squashed me with a look. "If you mean what I think you mean," she said archly, "you're wasting your time because everyone else thinks Daddy and I have produced a masterpiece. Mrs. Williams cried because she was so touched. She said it made her so happy to realize what good friends she had that even if she didn't get Othello it was worth it just to know that. Of course," she added, "that's negative thinking, because the play's going to be a success, and she is going to get Othello. I only wish Maxwell and Julian were taller. It's going to be an awful runty-looking horse."

"Why not use the real thing," I suggested, thinking I might as well try and be helpful since I was outnumbered. "There's always Horse."

"What, have her lean on everything and smash the scenery to bits! It's only going to be cheap plywood, you know." She tapped her teeth with a pencil. She was rewriting the first act for the seventh time. "No, they'll have to do. I think I'll ask Wallace's help. They should be able to design a nice horse's head at the art college, and maybe he could get some friends up to paint the scenery."

"Hey, wait a minute!" I cried gleefully, delighted at this chance to trip her up. "Haven't you forgotten Hamilton, your leading man? Don't tell me they finally have to meet. Well, let me know when, because I wouldn't miss it for the world. I mean two old family friends like that should be able to spend many a happy hour reminiscing about the good old days when they were young."

"Sadist!" she growled at me. Heaving a great sigh, she stared wistfully off into space beyond her typewriter. "It was bound to happen one day, of course. I shall lose one of them, if not both. But that's life. Tragedy enriches the soul."

I couldn't see that it would be such a great tragedy to lose either Hamilton or Wallace, even though I had buried the hatchet with both of them, but the rather uninteresting fact was that when they finally did meet, nothing happened at all. I think they were both so weird in their own ways, that each thought Margaret couldn't possibly be serious about the other. Margaret, who had been anticipating dramatic scenes of renunciation, had her nose put out of joint, but she had to swallow her disappointment and get on with her multitude of jobs. Besides being co-writer, she was also assistant director, dramatic coach, stage and costume designer, as well as an extra when needed, so she didn't have much time to enrich her soul by being tragic. That would have to wait till afterward.

Certainly there was nothing tragic about the play. Sometimes when we were rehearsing, we couldn't say our parts for laughing. It wasn't that the play was so funny. It was the people in it, like Hamilton with a ferocious moustache plastered to the upper lip of his cherub's face, painfully grinding out his lines in a flat monotone that drove even Margaret to distraction; and Kathy and Dinah made up to look pale and pasty, coughing consumptively and swooning in the most unlikely places. Mrs. Williams alone was fantastic, a born actress. She drifted serenely through all the chaos looking radiant in stage makeup as she held up banks, conned old ladies, all played by Grandma in different bonnets, and defended her virtue from Hamilton, who lost his moustache whenever he tried to give an imitation of passion. Wallace and his friends from art college had come up with a masterpiece of a horse's head. We stapled it to a moth-eaten old blanket and attached long strands for a tail. When Maxwell and Julian pranced about the stage, trying to coordinate their movements, the blanket was forever slipping sideways, exposing Maxwell's rear end, and as they were giggling most of the time and trying to stifle their giggles, the horse gave the impression it was suffering constantly from a severe case of indigestion.

It was a play to end all plays, all right, but what could you expect where Father and Margaret were involved? Mr. Archer and I took a back seat in the proceedings. We were given the tasks of prompting, scene shifting, and any of the other hundred and one things that kept turning up, but I admit we did have fun.

We decided to leave the opening date till the last possible moment as we needed all the rehearsal time we could get, which meant we would be putting it on during the first week in June, one week before Mr. Jones came back from Europe. We hoped the weather would be nice then, but if it wasn't, we had a tarpaulin all ready for a makeshift shelter.

There was nothing that Margaret and Father, between them, hadn't thought of. They ran off hundreds of posters, and we cycled and drove for miles around the countryside, pinning them up on every likely building and telephone pole we could find. There were going to be two performances on Saturday and one on Friday night, and we needed a lot of people if we were going to achieve our goal. We even made a trip into Kitchener and stuck up posters on the bulletin boards of supermarkets and drugstores. No publicity agent could have been more thorough than we were, but there was one thing we had all agreed upon. No one, not even Jim, who was giving me regular lessons on Queenie now and following the progress of the play with interest, was to know what we were doing it for. We were terrified that if Mr. Jones got an inkling of what was going on, he would grab Othello before he went to Europe, and all our hard work would have been for nothing.

By the end of May, Father assembled the cast together and announced that he was satisfied. The scenery had been painted by art students who arrived every weekend with pots of paint and vivid imaginations, led by Wallace who was in his element whenever he was concocting vile color schemes. The dirt floor of the original barn had been swept and scraped and tidied until you could almost have eaten off it, and the folding chairs, courtesy of Grandma and the minister, were in place. Even the programs were ready to be sold at five cents apiece. Mother and Margaret had been sewing night and day for weeks, doing marvels with scraps of materials to make costumes worthy of the play, and the final dress rehearsal had been run through successfully.

"I think you can all feel very proud of yourselves," Father said, giving us a last little pep talk. "We've really made something out of nothing here, and I couldn't have wished for a better group of performers to work with. I want to thank you all for your efforts, and I shall see you back here on Friday for opening night, when as we say in show business, may you all get out there and break a leg."

Mother sighed and whispered to me, "I wish he hadn't said that. Knowing you lot, someone's sure to take it literally."

I walked part of the way home with Kathy and Dinah and Mrs. Williams, and before I left them, she said to me, "You know, Joanna, this has been one of the happiest times of my life, and not just because we're doing it for Othello. It's been a heartwarming experience for me, and I think your family are wonderful people."

That made me feel terrific, and just for a moment I forgot all the shortcomings of my family and agreed with her wholeheartedly. There was another nice surprise for me when I got home. John was on the phone, calling from Florida.

"Hi, Funny Face," he said. "Just calling to let you know I'll be home some time on Friday, so you can get rid of all your other boyfriends."

He had a way of talking like that, which was wonderful for my ego. "Oh, that's great!" I squealed over the phone. "Then you'll be home in time for the play."

"What play?" he asked. "What are you up to now?"

"Margaret's play," I said. "The Old Barn Theater is having its grand opening on Friday night. Shall I save you a seat?"

He wanted to know more, but all I would tell him was to be over at our place by seven o'clock and he would be in for a surprise.

"Nothing you do would surprise me," he said. "But I'll be there. I miss you."

"I don't believe it," I said, "but it sounds nice, and I miss you, too."

Now everything was perfect for me. Friday dawned under a cloudless sky, and the weather forecast said absolutely no rain for three days. It was strange to come home from school and see the new sign on the gate saying THIS WAY TO THE OLD BARN THEATER, and arrows pointing down the yard. The cast had assembled early, and there were all sorts of minor panics going on. The dogs were beside themselves with excitement, so Mother told me to take them somewhere and get lost for a while, since all my jobs were superficial and I could be spared.

I walked slowly over the fields, watching the dogs nosing trails through the hedgerows, and thought how strange life was. It was nearly a year ago since I had fallen from Othello and thought my life was over. Now here I was teaching riding and loving it, jumping Queenie again, making my debut in show business, and actually feeling grateful to Othello for taking me on that wild ride last summer. Down in the paddocks, I left the dogs outside the big barn and went to see Horse and Othello, who had their quarters side by side. I shared a pocketful of sugar lumps, saving two extra for Horse who would always be our special horse; then I took Othello aside and said, "You're a great clodhopper of a horse, but you're very beautiful, and I think you've helped me to grow up. I'm very grateful to you. Now don't you worry about a thing. We've got everything in hand, and Mr. Jones will never get you."

Our gratitude didn't appear to be mutual. He punted his big square nose hard against my chest and sent me flying halfway down the barn, but I suppose that was just his way of showing affection.

I went back and found the worst of the panic was over. Instead everyone was going round in a dreadful state of despair because they couldn't remember a word of their lines, and the audience was already arriving. Pickup trucks and old cars were parked all along the driveway and down the road. One thing about people in rural areas, they are great for attending any social function from auction sales to flea markets, just so long as they can get together and exchange gossip. Wallace's friends were selling tickets at the door, while I was in charge of the P.A. system that Father had borrowed from the sound engineers at the television studios. The music was coming out satisfactorily, if somewhat squawky, so I decided to go around to the front and see if John had made an appearance. I walked down the aisle between the seats and who should I see coming in to the auditorium but John and Mr. Holmes! I just stood stock-still and gaped at them. John saw me first. He came down, put his arms round me and gave me a great big kiss, but all I could do was stare pop-eyed over his shoulder at his father.

"I see Margaret got her drama group launched," Mr. Holmes said to me with a smile. "John invited me over; otherwise I would never have known about it. You seem to be drawing a good crowd, and I must say the play has an intriguing title. I'm looking forward to seeing it."

I gulped and could hardly manage to raise a smile for John, but I hoped he would put it down to first-night nerves. As soon as I could escape, I dashed round to the cow shed and collared Margaret.

"He's here!" I cried distraught. "Mr. Holmes is here. He's come with John! I thought you said he wouldn't be interested in amateur dramatics. What are we going to do now?"

Margaret was more than a bit frazzled, and I was the last straw to her. Running her hands through her hair, she cried, "Oh Joanna, don't you start making scenes! That's all I need. People never recognize themselves as villains anyway, only as heroes, so I don't know what you're worried about. For heaven's sake go and look after the music. The record's going to end any minute. Can't I count on anybody around here to do what they're supposed to do?"

With no hope there, I slunk back to the wings and contemplated sadly the ups and downs of life, which seemed to be one gigantic seesaw.

The barn filled up, and eventually Margaret got everyone into some sort of order, and the play started. Looking back on it afterward, I suppose it must have been very funny, though I wasn't in the mood for it at the time, being so worried about what Mr. Holmes would think. Glassy-eyed and petrified with stage fright, Hamilton drifted through it in a daze, and we had to keep turning him around and pointing him, like a hound dog, in the right direction; and Kathy coughed so realistically in her first scene that she choked and had to be thumped on the back and given water from a disembodied arm which appeared, snakelike, from behind a backdrop. Maxwell and Julian were in their element as the horse, snorting and prancing around with such enthusiasm that the old floorboards rattled alarmingly. Mrs. Williams was superb, calm and unruffled, and improvising for everyone else when they forgot their lines. Wallace's friends, scattered throughout the audience, gave piercing catcalls and whistles whenever she appeared, and soon they had everyone in the auditorium joining in until it was like a madhouse, but they were all enjoying themselves tremendously, which I suppose was the most important thing.

Father joined me in the wings for the last act, his face flushed with success. "Well, Joanna," he said, "if the next two performances are as good as this one, Mrs. Williams has that horse in her pocket. That woman has missed her calling. She should have been on the stage."

She was on the stage right now, looking gorgeous in a wedding dress that Mother had run up from an old sheet, as she got hitched to Hamilton whose villainous moustache was decidedly at a 45-degree angle by this time. Maxwell and Julian were lurking, giggling, behind the scenery ready for their cue to leap onstage and carry Mrs. Williams off into the sunset along with Kathy and Dinah, but this time their enthusiasm went too far. With a tremendous bound they burst into the limelight; there was an ominous crack, and before our horrified eyes, the whole middle section of the stage collapsed. Hamilton saved himself by grabbing at the scenery, and Kathy and Dinah were to one side of the stage, but Mrs. Williams and the horse disappeared in a cloud of dust and debris into the old foundation beneath.

For a moment there was utter chaos and confusion; then suddenly Mr. Holmes was up on the stage, commanding everyone to remain in their seats and stay calm, while Father and John hauled Mrs. Williams, Maxwell, and Julian up from the gaping hole. Miraculously no one was hurt, but the beautiful work of art that had been the horse's head was smashed beyond recognition. Mrs. Williams' wedding dress that Mother had sewed so painstakingly was ripped and torn, and she was festooned in cobwebs from head to foot.

Once he was assured that there were no injuries beyond a few cuts and bruises, Mr. Holmes restored order to the audience, getting everyone to file out in an orderly fashion. The play had been almost over anyway, so no one felt cheated; in fact the spectacular finish was a bonus that they could talk about for weeks. The rest of us were too stunned to think logically, except for John, who suggested that we all go into the house and make a pot of tea to calm our shattered nerves.

It seemed like a good idea, and Grandma soon had the kettle on and the cups out, while the rest of us just sat around limply, too disheartened even to talk. We didn't have a theater now. All our weeks of work had literally crumbled into dust.

"What are we going to do?" wailed Margaret in anguish. "We've advertised two performances for tomorrow, and people are going to come, probably miles, and we'll have to turn them away!"

Mother did her best to console her. "The way news travels in the country, dear, I'm sure everyone will know what happened by tomorrow morning. And perhaps Daddy and Wallace can do the repairs between them, and we can put the play on again in a couple of weeks. It was such a success. I've been to a lot of plays in my life, but I've never seen an audience enjoy themselves more."

"But two weeks will be too late!" cried Kathy, almost in tears. "Mr. Jones will be back from Europe next week, and he'll buy Othello. And we had everything worked out so beautifully!"

Mrs. Williams put an arm around her. "Hush, dear, it doesn't really matter. We tried, and that's what counts.

Look what fun we've had. I—" She broke off suddenly and her mouth stayed open. We all turned and saw that unknown to us, Mr. Holmes had come into the kitchen with John, after directing the last of the cars off the property. They were looking at us curiously.

"What's all this about Othello and Mr. Jones?" asked Mr. Holmes. "Is this something I don't know about?"

It was Father who had to tell him, because the rest of us were tongue-tied. "I suppose it was my fault in a way, Jack," he said. "Mrs. Williams, here, is so fond of that horse of yours that she was just about heartbroken at the thought of not being able to go on riding him. Joanna wanted to ask you to keep him, but I forbade her to ask any more favors from you, so the only alternative seemed to be for Mrs. Williams to buy him herself, so we've all been trying to help her toward that end. The proceeds from this play tonight were going toward the purchase of Othello, but we appear to have a little setback on our hands."

"It wasn't meant to be you!" I exclaimed. I couldn't bottle it up any longer. "Mrs. Williams gave Margaret the idea for the play, but the villain wasn't meant to be you, honestly!"

Mr. Holmes looked a bit stupefied, and I couldn't blame him; but suddenly John beside him was laughing, and then he was laughing, too.

"My goodness, I should hope not. No offence meant, of course," he said with a twinkle in his eye to Hamilton, who still didn't appear to have come completely out of his daze. "May I join you?"

Remembering her manners, Mother rushed to bring two

more chairs to the table, and when Mr. Holmes and John were seated, Father said, "I'm sorry to have gotten you involved in this, Jack, but you know my family."

"I certainly do." Mr. Holmes didn't sound annoyed. His eyes ran around the table until they fixed on me, trying to scrunch down into my chair and become invisible. "I appreciate your father's concern, Joanna," he said, "but it wasn't really necessary. I think we're about equal where favors are concerned, and this riding school of yours has given me every bit as much pleasure as it has you, I'm sure of it. If you want to keep Othello in the school, well, then, that's perfectly all right with me. I'll tell Mr. Jones I've changed my mind about selling him."

I couldn't believe it. I just sat there with the tears running stupidly down my face, and grinned like an idiot. I wanted to run around the table to hug him, but then, to all our astonishments, Mrs. Williams, whom we had temporarily forgotten, beat me to it.

"Oh!" she said, throwing her arms around Mr. Holmes. "You wonderful, wonderful man!" Then, suddenly realizing what she had done in front of us all, she turned beet red, mumbled something about getting changed, and fled from the room. It was the one and only time since I had met Mrs. Williams that I had seen her up against a situation she was unable to cope with.

Eating Cake

SO THAT was how Othello became a permanent member of my riding school. Mrs. Williams said she would still like to own him one day, but meanwhile there was no hurry, because with all the money she had made, she could have riding lessons any time she wanted, without the worry of looking after him.

"When Dinah and I are grown up and are making money," Kathy confided in me, "we're going to buy him for Mommy and pay for him to be boarded at Holmwood Farms, so he'll get the best of care but really belong to her. Now she has to share him with other people."

"That's nice, Kathy," I said, smiling at her. "I guess you think your mother's pretty special, eh?"

She nodded emphatically. "Dinah and I think she's the best. We were kind of sorry for ourselves when we first came to live here, but now we think we're very lucky. Lots of children with two parents aren't so lucky as we are."

Remembering how insecure Kathy had been when I first met her, that made me feel good, and I felt pretty lucky myself to have them for friends. Unfortunately for Margaret, the future of the Old Barn Theater was not so happy. After examining the ruins of the stage, Father pronounced that it was irreparable. Margaret was quite distraught at first, but she got over it when Mother told her she ought to concentrate on writing plays, since she seemed to have a natural talent for making people laugh. I could have told her that a long time ago, but I'm not sure that Mother and I were talking about the same thing.

Hamilton, however, was very pleased that her amateur dramatics phase was over, and sometimes I couldn't help wondering if he had practiced a little sabotage on the quiet; but that wasn't fair of me because I don't think he had the brains to think that up. Anyway we had to drive all over the countryside again, pulling down our posters, and soon the short, glorious life of the Old Barn Theater was just a happy memory.

Several days later John and his father came down to the arena to watch Jim giving me my Saturday afternoon workout on Queenie. I was coming along nicely. My back never bothered me at all, and I was doing dressage and going over four-foot jumps with no ill effects. Jim still wasn't pushing me to the limit, and after half an hour, while John and I walked Queenie around the ring to cool her off, I saw him go into a huddle with Mr. Holmes. I suspected they might be discussing my progress, but I wasn't prepared when Mr. Holmes came up to me and said, "Well, Joanna, do you want to go back into training seriously? Jim says there's no reason now why you shouldn't. We could start entering you in shows at the end of this month, and if you're willing to work hard, and I do mean hard, I can't see why you shouldn't be eligible for the Royal Horse Show in November."

I was so startled I could only stare at him stupidly. They were all waiting for my reaction, expecting me to be overjoyed, and so I should have been, but something was wrong; I couldn't explain the feeling. I had been waiting for this moment since last July, and now I couldn't get worked up about it at all. I must have disappointed them badly, and I didn't know what was the matter with me. I forced myself to smile and say, "That's wonderful," but Jim knew me too well to be deceived.

"What's the matter, sweetheart? This isn't like you. The Joanna I know would be doing handsprings all over the arena at the good news."

I tried to hide my embarrassment by fiddling with Queenie's bridle. I was feeling clumsy and inarticulate. "It's so sort of sudden, I guess," I said. "I wasn't expecting it this year. I'll have to work awfully hard, won't I?"

Mr. Holmes gave me a strange look. "Hard work never scared you off before, Joanna. You used to be a devil for punishment. Have you lost confidence in your ability? If you have, that's understandable after this long time, but I can assure you that once you've entered a show again and come away with a couple of red ribbons, it'll be just as if you've never been away." He smiled at me reassuringly.

"If I didn't believe you could do it, I wouldn't let you try. You believe that, don't you?"

I nodded, touched by his faith in me. "Okay," I said. "But I'll have to give up the riding school, won't I? There won't be time for that anymore." And there it was, staring me straight in the face, the thing that was bothering me. I didn't want to give up the riding school. It was my own baby, my own special project, and I didn't want to give it up, not even for the chance of making a name for myself at the Royal. It was crazy, but there it was. Some of the happiest times of my life had been spent teaching other people to ride well, and the small achievements of my pupils were more heartwarming because they were shared than that lonely personal climb to glory that had so absorbed me last year.

Thank goodness, John was there, because he understood without my having to tell him. "Joanna's changed, Dad," he said quietly. "I don't mean she's lost her nerve; it's just that her values have changed. Isn't that right, Jo?"

I squirmed under the barrage of their inquiring looks. I felt so ungrateful I wanted to shrivel up into the sawdust. It was hard to put my feelings into words, but I made a faltering attempt:

"I do still want to ride Queenie in the Royal, Mr. Holmes. I really do, but it's just that I'm going to miss teaching at the school so much. It makes me feel so good to see kids like Kathy and Dinah, so scared and clumsy when they start, turning out to be competent riders and getting so much pleasure out of it. And it's because of me—because I helped them." That sounded terribly conceited to my ears, and I just gave up and cried out in despair, "Oh, I'm such a mess! I make such a mess of everything! I want to ride in the Royal, and I want to teach in the school, too, but if I ride in the Royal this year, I just won't have time to teach, because I'm so rusty I'll have to practice all my spare time!"

I really did feel then that I was a total disaster, and that very soon people would get sick to death of my contrary ways and wash their hands of me completely. I saw Mr. Holmes and Jim exchange pertinent looks, then Mr. Holmes said, "In other words, you want to eat your cake and have it, too. Is that right, Joanna?"

"I guess so," I mumbled miserably. "But that's not possible, is it?"

"Oh, I don't know." Something about my sorry plight seemed to be amusing Mr. Holmes. "What do you think, Jim?"

Jim put his head to one side, and squinted at me like a wise old bird. "Well, what I do think, Mr. Holmes, is that our Joanna has turned out all right, in spite of some moments of doubt on my part. And I'd say yes; in this case she can eat her cake and have it, too. For instance, what if she were to put off going into the Royal until next year, then we could take it nice and easy with the training, and it shouldn't interfere with her teaching at the school."

I looked at them, both smiling at me now as I stood beside Queenie, and I had to swallow a lump in my throat because they were both so kind and understanding and there wasn't any way I could ever tell them how dear they were to me.

"As a matter of fact, Joanna," said Mr. Holmes, "I would really prefer that you put it off for another year because the longer you wait, the stronger your back will become, with less chance of anything happening if you should have a tumble. But you were so disappointed last year, I talked it over with Jim, and we felt we ought to give you the chance if you wanted it."

"Then you don't really mind," I said with a catch in my voice.

He shook his head. "I've told you, Joanna, those days are over when another cup or ribbon was a matter of life and death to me."

"I'll win you a gold cup next year, I promise!"

He laughed. "Fair enough, Joanna, I'll keep you to that promise, and I'll expect to see some future Olympic riders turning out from those classes of yours. But you'll have to excuse me now, because I have a six o'clock appointment, and I rather think I'd better not be late."

I saw him exchange a mischievous glance with John, but I didn't think anything of it at the time. I was so full of my good luck, I really did want to turn those cartwheels and handsprings all over the arena now. John took my arm and said, "Let's go and look at that future champion of yours, Jo. I haven't seen him since I got back. Perhaps you'll get a gold medal on him one day."

"On Horse the Second?" I grinned back at him. "He's just like his mom. He'd rather have a sugar lump any day."

Holding hands, we left the paddocks and climbed the hilly fields where the first green sprouts of corn were already poking through the earth, and when we reached the hill, where we could look down on our house, I said to John, "Do you remember the first time I met you? You were sitting up here on Queenie, and I thought you were the luckiest person in the world. Boy, how I envied you!"

"And now?" he asked, putting his arms around me.

"Now," I said, "I think I'm the luckiest person in the world, and I don't envy anybody—not anybody at all."

"Good for you!" He released me and started down the hill. "Come on, I'll race you to the bottom!"

The wind carried us with it, and we practically hurtled down the hill, laughing with the joy of being alive on that beautiful June day. Horse the Second was feeling pretty good, too. He was kicking up his heels in the field and racing circles around Tangles, who was getting fatter and woollier and looked rather bored with the whole business. The dogs had come racing over from the yard to greet us, and out of the corner of my eye I could see Blob stalking spiders in the remains of the Old Barn Theater. There was a nice togetherness about seeing them all there, going about their own business, and yet belonging to us at the same time.

"I like my family," I said to John in a moment of intense affection for them. "Even the people part aren't bad."

John laughed, but he looked serious when he said, "Lots of people like your family, Jo. I'm sure I do, and my dad, and Mrs. Williams. By the way, I hope Dad doesn't keep her waiting. I've heard from Jim she can be quite a tyrant when she's annoyed."

It didn't sink in at first, but when it finally did, I whirled around on John and practically shrieked at him, "You mean your dad's going out with Mrs. Williams?"

He gave me an infuriatingly casual smile. "Didn't you know? I think he was really bowled over with her in that play, and he's always admired gutsy women. He told me how she stood up to him in the arena, even though she was wrong, and he admired that."

"He did?" I gulped.

"Yes, and she's a real good looker, isn't she? I think he's smitten."

I thought of Mrs. Williams in the kitchen up to her eyeballs in grease, and that awful apron and rubber gloves, but maybe Margaret was right after all; the mind did tend to obliterate the bad moments and only remember the good.

"What's the matter?" asked John, amused at my expression. "Don't you approve?"

"Nobody tells me anything!" I wailed. "Nobody tells me anything at all! I'm always the last to know."

"Can you wonder?" said John.

I wasn't quite sure what he meant by that, but I didn't think it was exactly complimentary. I didn't pursue the point further. To tell the truth, I was so bowled over at the idea of Mrs. Williams and Mr. Holmes going out together after our attempts at matchmaking had failed so miserably, that it took quite a while to register with me. When it did, I felt the laughter welling up inside me, but I managed to control it, although I couldn't help saying with a secret smile, "Maybe Dinah and Kathy won't need to buy Othello for their mother when they grow up, after all."

"What are you talking about now?" asked John.

"Nothing." I grinned, turning away. "Absolutely nothing."

"I don't believe you." He grabbed me and turned me

around. "I swear to God you're up to something again, Joanna. What is it?"

Looking at his distracted face, I couldn't keep the laughter down any longer. It bubbled up and spilled over. I felt the only way to hush him up was to kiss him, so I did.

"You still want to know?" I whispered in his ear.

"Never mind," he said, drawing me closer to him. "It's not important. It'll keep."